Wouldn't you know it?

The one guy in a long while who really turned her on would be someone who wanted to disappear into the bush on some wild-goose chase. Ivy started the helicopter's rotors and went through the preflight routine. They were airborne before she looked at Alex again.

His face was chalky and he was sweating, swallowing repeatedly. With the force of a blow it dawned on her that the man was terrified. *He was afraid of flying.* She should have recognized the signs earlier that day, but she'd been preoccupied with pointing out the landscape. She'd just expected him to love the experience as much as she did.

He didn't have his earphones on, so she couldn't reassure him. She reached over and touched his knee to get his attention and get him to put on the headset.

But he only pointed at the control panel, where smoke was curling out in slow wispy streams.

Dear Reader,

A Valentine's gift of a helicopter ride over the snowy mountains of Vancouver became the inspiration for this story. The pilot was a gorgeous young woman, and I knew I had the makings for a complex and interesting heroine. Then my brother and I decided to run away for a few weeks. We went north to Alaska on a long, meandering journey by car, and I fell in love with the vast countryside and the unique and generous people we met along the way.

This is the story of a search for personal freedom, which in the end is never satisfied by anything external. I believe that true freedom comes only when we understand that there's just one of us here, that learning to trust and to love one another on every level brings peace. And if along the way we find one special someone with whom to watch the northern lights–then we are truly blessed.

Please pay me a visit at www.bobbyhutchinson.com.

Much love, always,

Bobby

Past Lies

Bobby Hutchinson

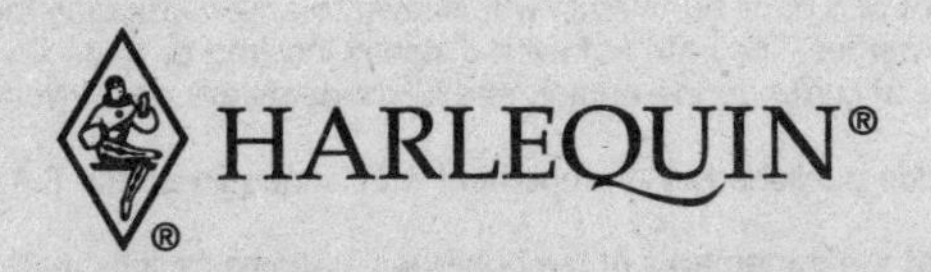

TORONTO • NEW YORK • LONDON
AMSTERDAM • PARIS • SYDNEY • HAMBURG
STOCKHOLM • ATHENS • TOKYO • MILAN • MADRID
PRAGUE • WARSAW • BUDAPEST • AUCKLAND

ISBN 0-373-71325-8

PAST LIES

This edition published by arrangement with Harlequin Books S.A.

www.eHarlequin.com

Printed in U.S.A.

Books by Bobby Hutchinson

HARLEQUIN SUPERROMANCE

166–SHELTERING BRIDGES
229–MEETING PLACE
253–DRAW DOWN THE MOON
284–NORTHERN KNIGHTS
337–A PATCH OF EARTH
376–REMEMBER ME
443–JOURNEY'S END
492–VAGABOND HEARTS
556–MAN, WOMAN AND CHILD
595–NOT QUITE AN ANGEL
643–EVERY MOVE YOU MAKE
723–SIDE EFFECTS
753–THE BABY DOCTOR
797–FALLING FOR THE DOCTOR
844–FAMILY PRACTICE
876–THE BABY TRUST
906–WOMAN IN THE MIRROR
925–FULL RECOVERY
1000–ALL SUMMER LONG "Temperature Rising"
1010–INTENSIVE CARING
1051–THE FAMILY DOCTOR
1124–VITAL SIGNS
1265–GOOD MEDICINE

Huge thanks to Bree McMurchy, who helped me understand the whys and hows of flight, and who nearly convinced me I should learn to fly a copter. So Bree, this one's for you. Wheel and soar high, my friend, and come back safe.

CHAPTER ONE

Well, here I am at last, the Final Frontier. The boat just dumped me off in Valdez—which, by the way, the natives here call Valldeeze. *A dude with a beard and an attitude corrected my pronunciation. Tell the sprout his old man's about to start off on the adventure of a lifetime.*

From letters written by Roy Nolan,
April, 1972

Valdez, Alaska
Present Day

BE THE HELICOPTER, and keep an eye on the torque gauge.

Ivy's dad had drilled those axioms into her head while teaching her to fly. Like a soundless litany, his rules flitted through her mind as the altimeter needle dropped and she expertly guided the Bell Jet Ranger toward her targeted landing spot high on La Grave Mountain.

Sure, she'd flown the Bell innumerable times. And yeah, she'd attended professional flight school. But it was still Tom's voice she heard as she systematically ticked off the details of her landing procedure.

Pay attention to the wind, watch your approach speed, beware a right crosswind—and never get cocky. Safety never takes a holiday.

The Ranger hovered and then settled with a gentle bump exactly where Ivy had planned to bring it down, the rotors kicking up clouds of snow. As the blades slowed and the white storm settled, Ivy squinted through her sunglasses against the blinding sunshine glinting off glaciers, sending up prisms of color.

Mid-April in Alaska meant that the temperature on La Grave was a chilly twenty below. There'd been thirty centimeters of new snow this week in the higher altitudes, and the skiing was reportedly fantastic.

Ivy didn't know that from personal experience. She skied cross-country and conservatively downhill, but there was no way she'd strap boards on and attempt the heart-stopping crevasses and perpendicular drops of these sheer mountain cliffs. Extreme sports struck her as ridiculously foolhardy, although of course she'd never say any such thing to these ski bums and their guide who'd paid her top dollar to ferry them up here.

"Okay, gentlemen, last stop. Everybody out." Ivy's voice sounded loud in her ears as the rotors slowed. She opened her door and balanced on a strut to help unload the men's equipment.

"Great flight, skipper. You free for dinner tonight, by any chance?"

Ivy smiled at Glen as the muscular giant from Lake Tahoe strapped on his skis. He'd been hitting on her the past couple of days. He was probably in his early thirties. She was only twenty-seven, but she'd already outgrown him. Glen was looking for the next thrill. He wanted new ranges, new mountains. New lovers.

She understood that, because she used to be just like Glen. But somewhere along the line, she'd changed. Now she was looking for—what?

Stability? Long-term? No simple answer came to mind. How come it was always easier to know what you didn't want than what you did?

"Sorry," she said as he looked at her hopefully over the top of his expensive sunglasses. "I have a standing date with my steady tonight, and for some reason he doesn't believe in sharing."

It was a white lie. Well, maybe it was more like a whopper. She did have a dinner date, but there was no steady guy. Definitely not. Although Dylan was starting to make assumptions about that, and it was time to set him straight.

Glen pretended he'd been stabbed in the heart and had to slowly pull out the knife. There was laughter and good-natured ribbing from the other two guys.

"I'll be waiting at the pickup point around three this aft. Try to keep the slippy side down, troopers."

The package they paid for through Raven Lodge included instruction from a certified Heli-Ski guide, drop-off by helicopter at the top of the mountain and pickup at a designated spot at the bottom.

With a flourish and a final wave, they were off, gliding through the powder like dancers. Ivy climbed back into the Ranger and began her preparations for takeoff, a smile on her lips.

This was always the best part of her job, this time alone in the copter after the customers were safely delivered to their destination. Now she could relax as she lifted off and skimmed over the breathtaking Chugach terrain, catching glimpses of sparkling lakes, soaring over row after row of tall glaciers. Ivy had been born in Alaska, and sometimes she imagined there was still an invisible umbilical cord stretching from her heart down to the soul of this wild and magical land.

"It's born in us, love of the land and the air," her father had once told her. "It's an addiction, but it's a good one."

She lifted the Bell up and over the final peak and began the descent to Valdez. As the ground came up to meet her, she could see her father standing outside the mobile trailer that served as an office for their company, Up And Away Adventures. Tall and barrel-chested, Tom Pierce was still ruggedly handsome and incredibly fit for a man nearly sixty years old.

She set the chopper down precisely in the center of the cement landing pad and shut the engine off. The rotors thwacked as they slowed, before finally stopping. Ivy pressed the flight idle stop button and rolled the twist grip to full closed position. Light switches, off. Battery switch, off.

Another mission accomplished, Captain.

HE WATCHED AS HIS daughter expertly landed the copter on the pad. When the rotors stilled and the motor died, Ivy opened the door and jumped down, her long, lean body as toned as any athlete's. She waved her blue-billed cap at him in greeting, then ran her fingers through the short, thick copper curls cut boyishly close to her scalp.

Ivy's mother had had hair that same color when he first met her, although now Frances had let hers go snowy-white. She wore her hair long, down past her shoulders. She styled it every morning with an artist's precision and an arsenal of equipment. Tom had always liked watching her.

Lately, though, she closed her bedroom door.

Ivy, now, she wasn't interested in gilding the lily, not that she needed to. She, too, was beautiful, although in a very different way than Frances.

Ivy didn't accentuate her looks or even seem to be aware of them, which of course drove her mother nuts. Under his mustache, Tom's narrow mouth curled into a small, enigmatic smile. Frances's makeup case was bigger than most suitcases, and all Ivy carried with her was a tube of stuff that kept her lips from chapping.

"Hey, Captain." Ivy smiled at him, her high, Slavic cheekbones an inheritance from his father's side of the family. Tom's sister, Caitlin, had them, too. But Ivy's hair and her wide-set apple-green eyes were gifts from her mother, reminding him, as always, of Frances when they'd first met.

Tom rubbed a hand absently across his chest, where the familiar tightness lodged whenever he thought about his wife.

"So what's happening?" Ivy looped a hand through his arm, and with an affectionate squeeze he trapped it against his side. She was only a couple inches shorter than his six-two. He'd long ago stopped caring that she automatically shortened her stride to accommodate his limp. The old leg injury was bothering him more than usual today, maybe a storm coming.

"We got any more charters lined up?"

"Nope, not for today. Might be some last-minute tourists, you never know." Tom shook his head. "Just got back myself, I took that load of supplies up and dropped it where those damn fool climbers wanted. No sign of them, although their tent was there. I buzzed around a few times, place was deserted."

"Probably halfway up the mountain," Ivy speculated. "Climbers wouldn't waste a morning like this waiting for their supplies to arrive."

"Maniacs, the lot of them."

"Yeah, well, as long as we keep our radical opinions to ourselves, Captain, they'll go on hiring us. And that's good for our bank balance."

"I can play nice guy with the best of them," he snorted. "Never pissed off a client yet."

"What a track record, keep up the good work."

Tom knew that visitors to Alaska often viewed him as an eccentric local character. He figured it didn't hurt their business at all.

She playfully punched his arm. "You're such a phony. Everybody knows there's a soft gummy center under that prickly surface."

Not everybody. He knew for a fact Frances didn't think so. Tom squeezed Ivy's arm a little tighter and changed the subject.

"I've got that lumber and insulation Theo ordered loaded on the boat."

Raven Lodge was in a remote bay accessible only by boat or plane. "I'll take it up to the lodge this afternoon if we don't get any last-minute business," Tom declared. "Theo really wants to get going on those new cabins. I hear he's hired some damned yahoo from down south to help him."

"Oh, yeah? And how'd he meet this yahoo?"

"Jerry down at the Anchor introduced them when

Theo was in town a couple days ago. Perfectly fine carpenters right around here—you'd think Theo would hire local."

"Everybody's working on the new hotel," she reminded him.

"Well, I hope this dude has more going for him than that so-called fishing guide from San Francisco Theo hired last year."

The idiot hadn't known his elbow from his ass. He'd somehow foundered a boat with four tourists out in the Sound. Just luck that another boat was nearby, or the lot of them would have died from hypothermia.

"Uncle Theo must have liked this current yahoo or he wouldn't have hired him."

Tom knew she was teasing him. He grunted. "Theo likes everybody, that's his biggest problem." It wasn't a criticism of his brother-in-law so much as a statement of fact.

Ivy laughed. "You'll get to judge the guy for yourself if you're taking the stuff out. I have to pick up my skiers around three, so I'll probably see you up there. You want a lift back with me?"

"If you're staying for supper. Caitlin told me to ask you. You open to that?"

"Darn, I can't tonight. I've got a date." Ivy wrinkled her nose.

"Then I'll stay over, bring the boat back in the morning." Tom grinned at her expression. "Date's that bad, huh? Would this be Doc Fredricks you're not excited about?" There were always men buzzing around Ivy, too many of them useless vagabonds from God only knew where. More than once he'd been tempted to scare them off, one way or the other. But the doc rated higher than most on Tom's private scale.

Fredricks was steady, he had a damned good job at the hospital. And it looked like he was going to settle in Valdez. Most telling of all, he'd managed to survive more than a few weeks with Ivy. Tom had to admit his daughter was fickle.

"Dylan, yeah."

"He's good people, Ivy. I hear he's buying property. Has plans to build a house in that fancy subdivision just outside town, somebody said."

She frowned and pretended to think about that. "I think he mentioned something about it."

"He's solid. You could do lots worse." He worried about her. He knew from personal experience that the world could be tough on women.

Ivy shrugged nonchalantly. "We're just friends."

"Friends, eh?" Tom gave her a look. "Sounds to me like it's one more case of nice guys finish last with you."

"You trying to marry me off, Captain?" He heard the mild reproof in her tone. He'd learned long ago that his daughter had a full share of her old man's stubbornness, and more than a touch of his quick temper.

"Nope, just want you to be happy, honey. Sometimes I figure you're confusing good guys with bad. You've got a hell of a trail of broken hearts underneath those boots of yours."

"These boots are made for breaking hearts," she growled, and he smiled beneath his mustache. "Is Mom going with you to the lodge?"

Tom shook his head and the smile vanished. "Can't. She's teaching her night-school class tonight." Besides, Ivy should know by now that her mother never visited the lodge. Frances did have a class tonight, makeup technique, wardrobe choices, hairstyling. Things she was good at.

All the things that bored Ivy cross-eyed.

Aeronautics, now, that got his daughter's attention.

He reached past her to open the door of the office, and the short, dark-haired young man behind the desk smiled and waved a hand.

"Hey, Bert, how's it going," Ivy signed.

Bert Ambrose was Tom's protégé. A naturally gifted mechanic, his dream was to learn to fly. But Bert had been born deaf, and he'd been told it was impossible for him to be a pilot. Tom knew better. With help from the Association of Deaf Pilots, Tom was teaching Bert to fly.

"Where's Kisha?" Ivy had learned rudimentary signs from the mechanic.

"Went to get us pizza." Bert's smile was so big, his narrow eyes almost disappeared. "Kisha loves pizza."

And Bert loves Kisha, poor sod. *These girls nowadays, too independent for their own good.* Ivy included.

Kisha Harris manned the phones and the radio, dealt with paperwork and was great on the computer. She'd set up a Web site for Up And Away, and talked Tom and Ivy into advertising on the Web. She was a wonderful employee, but she'd made it clear from the beginning that the job was strictly temporary for her. She'd watched *The Snow Walker* about two hundred times, and she was convinced she had what it took to be an actress.

Tom figured there weren't that many acting jobs for short, very round girls with absolutely no experience, but he'd been smart enough not to tell Kisha so. In the meantime, she flirted outrageously with poor Bert.

"Any calls since she left?" Ivy asked.

"Three," Bert said in his deep, atonal voice, signing the answer simultaneously. He kept track by watching the light on the phone's base. The messages would be on the machine.

Tom had worked out his own version of sign language, a combination of some of Bert's and a lot of what seemed logical to him. And he spoke up around the kid. Too many people mumbled.

"Come and have a look at temp gauge on the Beaver," Tom bellowed. "The engine's been running high."

IVY WATCHED THEM LEAVE, shaking her head and grinning to herself at the fact that Captain still figured if he talked loud enough, Bert would hear him. She pushed the button to replay the messages.

There was a request for helicopter transport from a group of Seattle skiers, and another from a German tourist for an aerial tour by floatplane. Ivy scribbled down the numbers.

The third call was from her mother, asking if Ivy could join her for lunch at Mike's Palace. Ivy spent a puzzled moment wondering what was up. She and Frances weren't exactly in the habit of lunching together.

She made the business calls first, arranging dates and deposits, recommending her aunt and uncle's remote fishing lodge, when asked for advice on accommodation. Usually June, July and August were the busiest tourist months, but lately there'd been increased volume in the less crowded shoulder seasons—late April, May and September. Up And Away was having the best April ever. At this rate, their dream of owning the Bell instead of leasing it would soon be a reality.

At last Ivy dialed her mother's number.

"Frances Pierce."

Ivy was accustomed to her mother's businesslike manner on the phone. "Hey, Mom, it's me."

"Ivy, hi. Are you free for lunch? I thought Mike's Palace, but if you'd rather go somewhere else—?"

"No, that sounds fine. See you there in fifteen, okay?"

Ivy hung up, wondering why she hadn't just come right out and asked Frances what she wanted. That way maybe they could have skipped lunch altogether.

She took a moment to wash her hands and face in the cramped bathroom. Dampening her fingers, she ran them through her hair to freshen the short curls that had been flattened under her hat. She was wearing her usual work uniform: blue jeans, sturdy Frye boots, a white button-down shirt under a navy pullover. She caught herself fussing and turned away from the mirror.

Why was it that the only time she was even marginally aware of how she looked was when she was around her mother? It was time she got over that.

Before she headed out the door she shrugged into the black Gore-Tex jacket with the company logo she and Tom had designed—the outline of a stylized plane with a *U* and an *A* superimposed on it. The cap had the same logo, and she plunked it on, remembering too late her efforts with her hair.

Oh, well. Around Frances, it was a lost cause anyway.

CHAPTER TWO

It seems a lot longer than a week since I left Bellingham. I miss you and the sprout a lot, I keep thinking about that night he was born. I figured for sure you were going to die, Linda. I never dreamed how much pain a woman goes through having a baby.

From letters written by Roy Nolan,
April, 1972

IT WAS A TYPICAL SPRING day for Valdez, sunny but chill with a sharp, brisk breeze blowing off the harbor. The huge snowbanks were gradually disappearing. Ivy drove her battered red pickup with the window down, breathing in the smell of the ocean.

Mike's Palace was just a short drive from the office, and Ivy pulled into a parking spot right beside her mother's SUV and headed into the cozy little restaurant. Mike's was popular with locals and tourists because it had the best lasagna around.

It also had a view of the harbor. The walls were

covered with old newspapers that told the story of Valdez all the way from the gold-rush days through the oil boom, including the earthquake, the disastrous oil spill and the more recent tourist boom.

"Hey, Ivy, how ya doin'?" Mike, the proprietor, was tall, bearded and sinister-looking because of a crooked nose and a jagged scar that angled across his cheekbone and nose. He liked to let people think it was from a brawl, but Ivy knew he'd gone headfirst through the windshield of a snowmobile.

He jerked a thumb at a table by the window. "Your mom's over there."

The room was way too small to miss anyone—as if anyone with even one eye in their head would ever miss Frances. Her wild halo of long, snowy-white hair gleamed like a beacon, curling out from her skull as if it had been electrified. The brilliant turquoise sweater she wore stood out like a jewel among the drab browns and grays of the other patrons. Frances looked like a peacock trapped by a crowd of seagulls, Ivy decided, as she wound her way among the crowded tables and sank into a chair.

Seagulls, and now one woodpecker. The comparison amused her.

"Hello, Ivy." Frances's voice suited her. It was husky and dramatic, with a refined sensuality and a faint hint of the Midwest in the consonants. "Glad you could make it." She smiled, her wide, voluptuous mouth revealing perfect white teeth. As usual, Ivy felt diminished by her mother's beauty.

"Slow day," Ivy said, taking a long, thirsty drink from the water glass beside her plate. "I took a group up the mountain early this morning, they're skiing down and then I'll fly them back to Uncle Theo's."

Frances nodded. "I talked to Caitlin the other day. She said Sage and Ben were due back today from that wildlife conference in Montana."

Ben was Ivy's cousin, Sage his wife. Caitlin and Theo had twin sons, Ben and Logan, ten years older than Ivy. Growing up, she'd idolized both of them and, during her teen years, she'd had a massive crush on Ben, the more charismatic of the two. Thank God maturity cured things like that.

Maturity and the realization that her handsome cousin's actions didn't always live up to his charm. His second wife was Ivy's best friend, and there were times when she felt Ben didn't deserve Sage.

"Dad's going over to the lodge for supper tonight." Ivy watched her mother's green eyes, wondering if Frances knew or even cared where Tom was spending the evening.

Frances nodded. "Yes, he told me." She glanced up and smiled again at the plump waitress. "Hi, Sally. I'll have the lasagna, spinach salad and a glass of chardonnay."

"Same for me." About the only thing she and

Frances had ever agreed on was food. Ivy had inherited her mother's metabolism as well as her appetite, which meant they both enjoyed staggering quantities of food without gaining an ounce.

Conversation faltered as Sally poured their wine—one glass wouldn't impair her ability to pilot—and then brought a basket of hot bread and, a few moments later, their salads.

After she left, the silence stretched painfully. Had there ever been a time when talking to her mother was spontaneous and easy? If there had, Ivy didn't remember it.

Frances sipped her wine and Ivy wondered if her mother was also searching for a common interest. "How's Bert making out with his flying lessons, Ivy?"

Good one, Mom. Neutral, uncomplicated.

"Dad says he's a natural." *And how come you're asking me? Don't you ever talk to Dad about anything besides the plumbing and the bank balance?*

"His younger sister, Becky, is taking my class. She wants to be a model."

Ivy's instinctive reaction was to shake her head. She fought to control her reaction, saying in a neutral tone, "You think she's got what it takes?"

Frances tipped her head to one side, considering. "She'll have to lose a lot of weight. She does have the height, and that unusual ethnic look is hot right now."

"So what look was hot when you were in the

business?" Ivy didn't really care, but it seemed a pretty safe thing to ask. Touchy areas with her mother were any discussions involving Tom, the need for makeup, a decent wardrobe or dicey situations encountered during flights. And Frances's childhood—now there was a real no-go zone.

"Exotic All-American farm girl?" Frances gave her characteristic little Gaelic shrug. "I really don't know. I was lucky, because whatever it was, I seemed to have it."

"You sure did." Ivy thought of the stacks of fashion magazines carefully filed away in protective plastic, each featuring her mother on the cover. *The incomparable Francesca,* one photographer had labeled her. She'd been one of the first fashion models to become so famous they were recognized by just one name—and their beauty, of course. Francesca was one of the first supermodels.

Sally served their lasagna, and they ate hungrily for a few moments.

"You ever miss it, Mom? The…the glamour, the excitement?" It was something Ivy had often wondered but never dared ask, which was ridiculous. Her mother had made it clear early on that she didn't want to discuss certain aspects of her life, and Ivy was never sure what they were.

And when she was younger, Ivy had been scared that questions like this one would send Frances spiraling back into the depression that had ruled their household during Ivy's childhood. Frances was better now, but the painful memories were still there for Ivy.

Why her mother had chosen to leave her modeling life to marry Tom and live in Alaska had always been a mystery to Ivy, and probably to most of the inhabitants of Valdez as well. It was a small town, and nobody's private issues were usually sacred. That one, however, seemed to be.

Frances didn't respond right away, and Ivy figured she probably wasn't going to. Her mother had turned her head and was staring out the window. Her wide eyes were unfocussed, so she probably wasn't seeing the dozens of fishing boats in the harbor or the spectacular peaks of the icy glaciers that cradled the town.

Ivy buttered a chunk of sourdough bread and chewed stoically. *One small misstep on my part, one giant silence on hers.*

And then Frances actually answered. "It's not the glamour or excitement I miss—they're highly overrated in the world of high fashion," she said slowly. "A lot of it's grueling hard work, freezing your butt off modeling swimsuits in January, roasting to death wearing layers of winter clothes in July."

Ivy had always suspected as much, but Frances had never explained it before.

Frances's voice was thoughtful. "I think what I miss sometimes is the sense of being at the epicenter of everything—fashion, publishing, knowing ahead of time what a certain designer is going to feature in his next show, who the current darling of the art world is, what's happening to hemlines, shoulders, what era is in vogue. I get lonely for things like that, for haute couture." Frances glanced around the crowded room before leaning in. "And also for a suitable place to wear it."

Even Ivy, style challenged as she was, knew that Valdez wasn't the fashion capital of the western world. She didn't know one designer from another, and she certainly didn't care about hemlines or shoulders. In her opinion, the Alaskan environment provided art for free—glaciers, northern lights, mountain lakes in the summer dawn. As for clothing, well, she did have more clothes than the average woman, only because Frances had always insisted on Ivy having what she called a basic wardrobe.

That always included a black dress, a classic wool coat, well-cut pants and matching jacket, several lined wool skirts, a stack of cashmere sweaters and various silk, cotton and linen pieces for summer.

For years, Frances had consistently given Ivy one or two such useless items every birthday and Christmas, even when what Ivy really wanted were leather jackets, heavy boots and billed caps.

The clothing, expensive and timeless, took up

space in the back of Ivy's closet and filled several dresser drawers, ignored for the most part. She only yanked them out when she needed something to wear to a wedding, a funeral or a christening—one of those rare events in Valdez when jeans and a T-shirt or flannel shirt just wouldn't cut it.

Frances must have recognized the bemused expression on Ivy's face, because she laughed, a low, rich sound that made several people turn their way and smile in appreciation.

"Sure, I miss New York," Frances confessed. "The sophistication, the mistaken but pervasive belief that it's the hub of the world. Attitude, I guess you'd call it. I miss New York attitude."

Ivy drawled, "So, you figure we ain't got attitude up here in the 49th?"

"Plenty of it. Just not the same type." They ate for several moments and then Frances said, "What would you miss if you moved away from Valdez, Ivy?"

Ivy thought about it for a moment. She also thought what a strange conversation this was turning out to be. Normally she and Frances talked about the weather, food, recipes, the latest news item. Which was pretty limited and meant that they quickly ran out of things to say.

"I can't even imagine moving away. Oh, from Valdez, maybe, but not ever from Alaska. It's where I belong, it's in my blood." Curiosity got the better of Ivy. “Is that how you felt about New York, Mom? That it was in your blood?”

“No.” This time Frances didn’t hesitate. “I’ve never had that feeling about anywhere I’ve lived.”

“Not…not even your hometown?” Frances had grown up in a small town in southern Ohio, but that was about all Ivy knew. Frances never spoke of her childhood, except to say that her parents were dead and she had no relatives she wished to contact. “Didn’t you miss Brigham Falls when you left?” As soon as the words were out, Ivy realized she’d gone too far.

“Never.” Frances bit off the word as if it burned her lips. She pushed her plate away even though she wasn’t finished. “Now, are we going to have dessert?” Without waiting for a reply, she motioned Sally over.

Ivy felt heat rise in her face at the rebuff. She felt like a child being reprimanded. *Smack. End of discussion.*

You’d think by now she’d know better than to ask Frances anything really personal. But for a few minutes there she’d been seduced into thinking that she and her mother were communicating.

The hurt was nothing new. Except now Frances no longer retreated to the bedroom for days or sometimes weeks, while Ivy berated herself for making her mother sick.

“I’m having lemon meringue pie and coffee, please, Sally. What would you like, Ivy?”

"I have to take off. I have to do some stuff at the office and then I need to pick up my clients." Ivy pulled her wallet out and tossed several bills on the table beside her plate. She avoided looking at her mother.

"Please, Ivy, lunch is my treat." Frances tried to hand the money back. "I invited you."

"Next time." Which might be when the Columbia Glacier melted away to nothing. Ivy got up and shrugged on her jacket. "See you, Mom."

She hurried out the door without a backward glance, drawing in a shaky lungful of fresh, cool air as she headed to her truck.

More often than not, being around her mother left her resentful, shut out and confused. There was a line by Kipling, "and never the twain shall meet." It could have been written with her and Frances in mind.

CHAPTER THREE

If Alaska's all they claim it is, maybe you and I and the sprout could homestead up there, make a claim on a piece of land. This guy on the boat who's going up there to do that says land's still cheap in Alaska. I'll know better after I get there.

From letters written by Roy Nolan,
April, 1972

BACK IN THE RESTAURANT Frances's shoulders slumped in defeat. She'd thought that things were going well for once, that she and Ivy were actually connecting. And then, without warning, her daughter did that closing down thing she'd perfected as a young teen, eyes shuttered, mouth set, face like a thunderbolt.

Frances hadn't even had a chance to hint at what she really wanted to discuss with her daughter. She'd asked Tom if he'd break the news to Ivy, but she couldn't fathom what had ever made her think he'd take the initiative. When it came to emotional issues, avoidance was Tom's only coping technique. That, and projection. He found fault with other things to avoid looking at himself. She'd only realized that recently.

It was always easier to see the mistakes someone else was making. Several years of good therapy had at least given her some insight into herself, but it was still difficult not to blame Tom for the gaping holes in their marriage.

Sally appeared, setting down the lemon meringue pie and pouring coffee.

"Thanks." Frances forced a smile to her lips. "Your hair looks wonderful, by the way."

The girl had attended one of Frances's night-school classes, and her plain face lit up at the compliment. "Oh, thank you, Ms. Pierce. I had it cut in Anchorage. There's a new salon there, it's called Suki's." Sally's smile made her beautiful. "Enjoy your pie."

Frances had no appetite for the dessert now, or coffee, either. When Sally moved away, she messed up the pie with her fork, stirred cream into the coffee, and gazed blindly out the window, not seeing the Norman Rockwell harbor.

After years of depression, which at times left her inert, she was finally taking control of her life. She had a chance at a job in New York, teaching aspiring models. She was leaving Valdez. *Leaving Tom, leaving her marriage.* The decision had been a long time coming, but once she'd made up her mind, she couldn't believe she'd stayed here so long.

But she knew why she had. *Fear. Depression.* The conviction that all she'd ever had to offer was youth and beauty. And for years, she'd thought that she and Tom might still resolve their differences, recapture the connection they'd once shared. It had been powerful in the beginning.

Outside the window, a couple walked past with a small blond girl holding their hands. Every couple of steps, she drew her legs up, and the man and woman laughed and swung her between them like a pendulum.

Had she and Tom ever swung Ivy that way? She doubted it.

She'd been ill when Ivy was that age—it was only now, years after the worst of it, that she recognized depression as an illness. Before, she'd seen it as shameful weakness. Tom had taken over Ivy's care. And she'd become her father's girl, devoted to him, fierce in his defense.

Ivy would blame Frances for the marriage ending. She wouldn't understand why Frances had to leave, any more than Tom did.

She'd already lost a son. Jacob had died twenty-five years ago this month, on a rainy, cold Tuesday night. But the dimpled little boy was as fresh in her mind as ever. The pain of his loss had dulled with time, but it was still there. Was the price of freedom, of leaving Tom, to be the loss of her daughter as well?

"Ms. Pierce?"

Frances jumped. Sally was standing beside her.

"Sorry, I was daydreaming."

"Ms. Pierce, that man over there..." Sally tipped her head and rolled her eyes toward a balding man wearing a Western-style shirt, sitting alone at a nearby table. When Frances looked over, he smiled, gave a little bow and a wave.

"...He says he's buying your lunch, Ms. Pierce. I told him you were married, but he's real determined. Said you were the prettiest thing he's seen since he came up here." She bent over and hissed, "He's had a snootful, you want me to get Mike?"

"No need, I'm going now. Ivy left that." Frances pointed over at the money, more than adequate for their bill and a generous tip. She gathered up her coat and bag and got to her feet, conscious that the man was watching her every move. "Thanks, Sally. See you again soon."

Attracting men wasn't unusual. Ordinarily, Frances would walk away, careful not to look at the man, hideously self-conscious.

Today, however, some impulse made her stop at his table. Flustered now, he shoved his chair back and started to get to his feet. Frances said in a pleasant tone, "Please don't get up. I just wanted you to know that my husband is large, insanely jealous and violent. You really don't want to make him angry, do you?"

She walked out, aware that his bloodshot eyes weren't the only ones following her progress. She was trembling by the time she climbed in her SUV. She closed the door and rested her head on the steering wheel, and then she started to giggle.

She'd been afraid of going to New York, living on her own. She'd relied on Tom for so many years, she had no confidence in her ability to fend for herself. She knew the way she looked attracted unwanted attention. How would she deal with that?

Now she knew exactly how. She'd remembered some of her New York chutzpah, and she was going to do just fine. She'd made the right decision after all. She found her sunglasses and started the engine.

THROUGH WATER-STAINED glasses, Alex Ladrovik watched the green wake foam past the bow of the small aluminum boat, anxiously wondering if he'd made a huge mistake. He'd agreed on the spur of the moment to go to some remote fishing lodge to build two cabins before finding out the place was only accessible by floatplane or by boat. He'd had to entrust his beloved Jeep to a questionable parking garage in Valdez, and he was having second thoughts about the whole undertaking.

The boat ride was a rough one, waves slapping against the hull, salt spray half blinding him, but he was fine in boats, even those loaded to the gunwales like this one. It was only airplanes he had a phobia about.

"Raven Lodge is just around that next bend," Oliver Brady called out. The young fishing guide had met Alex on the dock promptly at noon, just as Theo Galloway had promised. They'd loaded Alex's gear, stacking it on top of lumber, cases of canned goods and boxes of fresh produce. They'd been chugging through the waves for a good half hour. It was a relief to know they would soon reach their destination.

Almost there, Anne Marie. Not that I have the vaguest idea where there is. Alex touched the breast pocket of his waterproof jacket, checking to make sure his daughter's photo was dry and tucked well down. He'd fallen into the habit of talking to her picture, which he'd clipped to the visor of the Jeep two weeks ago when he left San Diego.

The trip north had been long, and commenting out loud to Annie about the landscape and the day's events made it somehow less lonely. If it also made him a total whack job, well, there was no one to judge him except himself.

"There's the lodge," Oliver yelled as the boat rounded the point.

Alex caught his breath at the spectacular view, and he whistled long and low. "Now that's impressive." He squinted through salt-spattered lenses, and then took his glasses off and wiped them on a bandana he kept in his pocket for exactly that purpose. He shoved them back on his nose and sat forward, studying the place where he'd be spending the next few weeks.

Raven Lodge was on a spit of land that extended out into a narrow bay. The majestic, snow-covered Chugach Mountains rising from Prince William Sound formed a dramatic and formidable backdrop for the rustic two-story, rambling log structure and its impressive assortment of outbuildings. The whole place looked tidy and well cared for.

A long dock extended into the water, and several large boathouses undoubtedly sheltered numerous fishing boats, like the one they were riding in, which were needed to carry guests out into the Sound to catch the fabled king salmon, halibut and Chinook native to these waters.

Some distance from the buildings was a large cement pad.

"That's where the copter lands," Oliver explained. "Lots of skiers staying at the lodge, they get shuttled up the mountain in the morning and brought back at night."

Cabins were scattered among thick stands of Sitka spruce and western hemlock, and Alex caught sight of another, smaller log house, also two stories, some distance from the main building.

"That's where Ben Galloway and his wife live. Ben's one of Theo's boys," Oliver explained as they drew closer to the dock. "He's got a twin brother in Seattle, a lawyer. They're both nice guys."

Alex appreciated the input. "That's where Grace and I stay." Oliver pointed out two long, white clapboard bunkhouses nestled in a grove of pine trees. "You can bunk in with us or use one of the small cabins. Most of the guests stay right in the lodge this early in the season."

Oliver had told Alex how he and his longtime girlfriend had come north hoping to homestead. "We need a grubstake, so we're both working as fishing guides for the summer. Grace is a real smart woman. Can turn her hand to almost anything. I'm real lucky, finding her," he'd boasted with a grin that made Alex lonely for an instant.

"So, Alex, you think maybe you'll stick around?"

"I think I lucked out," Alex said. "Looks like a great place to work for a couple weeks."

"It is. And you couldn't have a better boss than Theo," Oliver declared. "Fair as they come. His wife Caitlin is a fantastic cook. Best grub I've ever had at a fishing camp. And they pay well and on time. A lot of places up here only offer minimum wage. The Galloways are good to work for."

Alex was relieved to hear it, although his reasons for taking the job hadn't been financial. Money was the least of his concerns. Idleness was his worst nightmare. He needed something to do, something physically exhausting and challenging enough to dull the sense of failure and loss that plagued him when he tried to sleep. Hard work was the only cure he'd found for insomnia.

Oliver pulled smoothly up to the dock and tossed a rope to Theo, who'd come hurrying down the walkway. Theo was a stocky, middle-aged man. Clean-shaven and ruddy-faced, he had a shock of snowy hair. The pipe stuck in the corner of his mouth looked as if it grew there.

He secured the rope and called out, "Welcome to Raven Lodge, Alex."

Alex clambered up to the dock and shook Theo's work-hardened hand. "It's a pleasure to be here, sir."

The other man laughed. "Theo is fine. We don't stand much on ceremony in these parts."

Alex helped the two unload the boat, and when all the supplies were stacked on the dock, Theo said, "Come on up to the lodge and meet Caity, then later we'll bring your gear up and get you settled."

Alex walked beside the older man, breathing in the sharp odor of salt water mingled with the smell of pine tree resin and wood smoke. Halfway up the long flight of stairs he tapped his breast pocket.

We're a long way from San Diego, Annie. He looked past the buildings at the dark, thick forest that surrounded this small patch of civilization. That's where he'd be heading soon. Into the wilderness. He shivered with a sense of foreboding.

So this is where it begins, where I find out once and for all what I'm really made of. He followed Theo up the wide wooden steps, noting with a carpenter's eye that they were each hewn out of one huge log.

Or maybe this is where it ends. Had he come up here to die? The thought wasn't frightening. Rather, it held the promise of peace.

Whichever it was, Alex knew that his life was once again abruptly changing direction.

CHAPTER FOUR

It's never bothered me much, not having family I could count on. You and I have that in common, eh, Linda?

From letters written by Roy Nolan,
April, 1972

"ALEX LADROVIK, meet my brother-in-law, Tom Pierce. Tom is Caity's older brother."

Tom had just arrived at the dock, and the men were standing beside a long wooden boat loaded with building supplies neatly covered by a blue tarp.

"Alex's up from San Diego," Theo added for Tom's sake. "He just got to the lodge a couple hours ago, caught a ride with Oliver and the groceries."

"How d'ya do." Tom didn't offer his hand and Alex decided against holding out his. He was aware that the mustached man was assessing him with cool gray eyes set in a weathered, still handsome face.

"Guess that's your green Jeep with the California plates, parked back in town in Olaf's garage?"

"She's mine, all right." Alex hoped his mud splattered, battered vehicle, would still be there when he went back to claim it. It had performed valiantly, never once breaking down on the long and often isolated journey.

"California," Tom said, making it sound like a third world war zone. "So what brings you to Alaska?"

"Adventure," Alex replied, giving the same explanation he'd used all along the way. "The job I had in San Diego ended, and I decided it was time to travel. When the weather warms up I want to hike into the bush, live off the land a while. Till then, I need a job."

That was true enough, although it didn't begin to really explain why he was here. Best to keep that to himself for the time being. No point in revealing your underbelly right away, especially since Tom didn't seem nearly as friendly as his brother-in-law. Maybe it just took him longer to warm up to strangers.

Tom's gaze flicked up and down Alex's long, rangy frame. "The bush, huh? You done much backcountry hiking on your own?"

"Some. Well, truthfully, not much. But I plan to do some extensive research before I head off."

"Research, now that'll impress the grizzlies." The derogatory snort and look Tom shot his way made Alex doubly glad he'd held back some of his personal info.

"Going off into the bush on your lonesome is one

fine way to end up dead," Tom said emphatically. "Every year we spend valuable time searching for damn fool adventurers gone missing. More people go missing up here than anywhere else in the U.S. Dumb thing to do, in my opinion. "

Out of politeness, Alex didn't mention that he hadn't asked for Tom's opinion. The older man was making his hackles rise.

Theo ignored Tom's outburst. Instead, he pointed at one of the outbuildings. "Let's stack the lumber in that shed over there, don't want it getting wet. If you move the boat down the dock a ways, Tom, we can get it unloaded."

Alex noticed that Tom had a pronounced limp, but otherwise his wide body was muscular and fit. He handled the two-by-fours and bags of cement almost as easily as Alex. The injury to his leg sure didn't slow him down at all.

Theo, however, was soon red-faced and winded. Without being obvious about it, Alex made sure he shouldered the heaviest of the materials. In a short while, they had the lumber, nails and bags of cement mix stowed inside the shed.

Theo wiped the sweat from his forehead with the arm of his blue flannel shirt. "I hate to admit it, but I'm out of shape. Way too much sitting around in the wintertime. Come on inside, you two. Caity's making supper and we deserve a drink."

Theo led the way. Inside the wide front doors of the sprawling log building, Alex glanced at the framed photos lining both walls he'd noticed earlier. There were color snapshots of smiling guests holding trophy fish, but there were also older black-and-white shots of men and women wearing clothing from the turn of the century. But he was quickly distracted by the wonderful smells that wafted down the long hallway from the direction of the kitchen, and he sniffed in hungry anticipation.

"Caity, love, Tom's here," Theo bellowed and within moments Caitlin Galloway came hurrying along the long hall to meet them, her handsome face wreathed in smiles. Her white hair piled on top of her head, she wore a white bibbed apron to protect her snug blue jeans.

She was attractive, not just physically—although she had glowing skin and a figure much younger women might envy—but also because of her warmth and kindness. Now he noticed that she had the same high cheekbones and gray eyes as her brother.

Earlier, she'd led him to the kitchen where a compact, ageless little woman was busy rolling and then flopping dough into eight pie plates. Her back was to Alex, and at first he saw only thick, inky black hair, braided and rolled into a knot.

"Mavis Armitage, meet Alex Ladrovik. He's the one going to build the cabins for Theo," Caitlin had announced. "We eat breakfast and dinner with the guests, but we usually have lunch here in the kitchen."

When Mavis turned, Alex had tried to hide his shock at the sight of her disfigured face. He'd seen burn victims, and he guessed that was likely what had left the puckered scars and discolored flesh that marred one side of her face and extended down her neck.

"Pleased to meet you, Mavis." Alex had smiled at the older woman and extended his hand. The defensive expression in her eyes told him she'd noticed his first involuntary reaction.

"Can't you see I'm up to my eyeballs in pie dough here?" She turned back to her work without another word. Mavis obviously wasn't anyone to mess with.

Those pies were baking now. Alex could smell the cinnamon and apples. His stomach grumbled and his mouth watered.

Caitlin gave her brother an exuberant hug and kissed his cheek. "Is Ivy going to stay and have supper with us?"

"Not tonight. She'll be here in a while delivering your skiers, but she can't make it for supper," Tom said. "She has a date."

"Oh, *too* bad for us. That young doctor?"

Tom nodded.

"Sage was looking forward to a visit with her," Caitlin said. "Well, there's always a next time. Now, if you men want to make yourselves comfortable in the living room, Mavis and I'll finish up in the kitchen and then I'll join you for a drink."

A few moments later, Alex was admiring the massive tumble rock fireplace that dominated one wall of the large living room. Above it was an oil painting of a handsome couple. Here, too, the clothing indicated that the painting was probably turn-of-the-century.

"Relatives?" Alex gestured at the painting.

"My grandmother and grandfather," Theo said.

"This whole place is remarkable," Alex commented, running a hand over a rough-hewn beam. "How long have you lived here, Theo?"

"All my life. I was born here and so was my father." Theo indicated the painting with a wave of his hand. "That's his father, William Galloway. He built the place. Raven's been in the Galloway family since the turn of the century."

Alex was impressed. "How did your ancestors come to settle here?"

"We'll have lots of time for that when we're working on the cabins," Theo said. "Right now, it's time for a drink."

"Families don't stay put anymore," Tom grumbled. "Everybody's got itchy feet, coming and going all over the place. Don't know what they're all looking for that they can't find at home."

Alex wondered if that was yet another poke in his direction.

"Not me and Caity," Theo said. "We never wanted

to be anywhere but here. Still don't." He opened the door of a tall highboy, revealing a well-equipped bar. "Tom, I know your poison. Alex, how about you? Rye, rum, beer?"

"A beer would be great," Alex said, and Theo handed him a bottle and a glass and then poured rye for himself and Tom.

The older men, glasses in hand, each took one of the deep armchairs that flanked the worn leather sofa. Alex sank into its soft cushions. He poured his beer and took a grateful sip, listening to the easy flow of family conversation.

"You and Ivy keeping busy, Tom?"

"Not bad at all. Way better than last year. Seems we're getting more tourists in April than we've had before."

Theo nodded. "We're noticing the same thing. We're fully booked for April and May, and then right through to September." Theo turned to Alex. "Tom and his daughter run a flight service in Valdez called Up And Away. Tom has his own floatplane, the Beaver, and Ivy flies a Bell Ranger. We've started doing package tours for skiers—they stay here and Tom or Ivy flies them up the slopes. You a skier, Alex?"

"I've never tried, never wanted to. I was never much good at sports." And the very thought of being ferried up a mountain by helicopter made him queasy. He couldn't help but wonder what type of woman would choose to be a pilot. He boarded planes only out of dire necessity, getting miserably airsick and hating every moment his feet were off the ground. "Did your daughter learn to fly in the military, Tom?"

"Nope, I did. Vietnam." He tapped his right thigh. "Shrapnel left me with a bum leg." He paused as a loud whirring announced the arrival of a helicopter. "That'll be Ivy," he said, and Alex noted the way his voice softened and his weathered, stern features softened.

A few moments later Caitlin walked in, her arm around a tall young woman's slender waist.

"Hey, Ivy honey, good to see you," Theo said, getting to his feet and embracing her. "How's my favorite niece?"

"About as fine as my favorite uncle." She waved a hand in Tom's direction. "Hey, Captain, long time no see." Then she turned curiously to Alex. "Hi there," she said with a wide, welcoming smile.

"Alex Ladrovik, my niece, Ivy Pierce," Caitlin introduced.

"How do you do, Ivy?" Alex stood as she came toward him with her hand outstretched. They were close to the same height, which put her just over six feet.

"Pleased to meet you, Alex. Ladrovik, have I got that right?"

When he nodded, she said, "That's an unusual name. Russian?"

"Yes, originally." Alex had taken her strong hand in his, feeling more than a little disconcerted by the initial effect she was having on him.

Ivy would stand out in any surroundings, and not just because of her height. There was something magnetic about her. He found it difficult to look anywhere else.

"We have a lot of people of Russian heritage in Alaska. So where are you from, Alex?"

"San Diego." She wasn't exactly movie-star beautiful. Her father's straight, narrow nose was perhaps a little too long on her. She had his high, elegant cheekbones, accentuating a squarish face. Her full, lush mouth was a trifle wide above a strong, no-nonsense jawline. And her hair gleamed like polished copper. Thick and curly, it was cropped shorter than his, clinging close to her elegant, narrow head. She had clear golden skin, translucent in the firelight, but her most arresting feature was her eyes. They were a peculiar shade of light green, the color of the Granny Smith apples his mother had always preferred for pies, and they were framed by long dark lashes.

"Think you'll like it north of 60, Alex?"

He had to stop staring at her. "I'm sure I will."

She was giving him a teasing smile, and a certain look in those unusual eyes told him she was probably accustomed to men gaping at her.

He was also still holding her hand. He dropped it abruptly.

"I hear you're a carpenter." She had a deep, husky voice with an intriguing catch in it. "Dad tells me you're going to build those new cabins Uncle Theo has his heart set on."

He dragged his eyes away from her and looked over at Theo, who seemed much more amused by Ivy's obvious effect on him than her father, who looked decidedly grim. "I'm going to give it my best shot."

"And we're starting at daybreak tomorrow," Theo said. "Gotta make hay while the sun shines."

"Don't let him scare you," Ivy said to Alex. "Daybreak in April isn't all that early up here. Certainly not like daybreak in July."

"That would be about two or three a.m., right?"

Theo chuckled. "Earlier than that. That's why they call this the land of the midnight sun." Theo was pouring white wine for Caitlin, who'd sat on the sofa. He waved a stemmed glass in Ivy's direction. "You want something to drink, honey?"

"No thanks, I've got to get back to Valdez. I want to say hi to Sage first, though."

"She'll be pleased to see you." Caitlin lowered her voice. "And you'd better pop in to the kitchen and say hello to Mavis, you know how easy she gets her feelings hurt."

"Far be it from me to get in her bad books," Ivy said with a grin. "Is Sage over at the house, Auntie, or is she upstairs in the office?"

"She's at home."

"I'll head over there, then. Nice meeting you, Alex." Ivy smiled at him before stooping over to smack a kiss on her aunt's cheek. "See you soon, Auntie. Don't get up, I'll go say hi to Mavis and then scoot out the kitchen door."

She started to leave and then turned back to her father. "Almost forgot. Dad, the skiers want to go up the mountain again in the morning. Will you be back in time to take those honeymooners up to the cabin on the Catella River? They'll be at the office at eight."

"No worries, I'll be there. I'm heading back at daybreak," Tom assured her. "See you in the morning, Ivy."

She raised her hand in a small salute. When she was gone, Alex felt as if the room had deflated a little, like a balloon losing some of its air.

He made a mental note to keep his distance from Ivy Pierce.

CHAPTER FIVE

Linda, I'm sorry I lost it when you told me about the baby. I was just shit scared, is all. Responsibility's never been my strong suit. Still isn't, or I wouldn't be on this cruddy freighter heading for the land of the midnight sun. I wanted you to know that now that the baby's here, I'm glad you didn't go to that doc the way I wanted you to.

From letters written by Roy Nolan,
April, 1972

TEN MINUTES AFTER Ivy left, Caitlin sipped the last of her wine and got briskly to her feet. "The guests are washing up, so we'll eat in half an hour."

"If you'll excuse me, I'd like to clean up a little too," Alex said.

"Don't bother with your tux tonight, lad." Theo grinned at him. "We're only semiformal around here."

"Glad you warned me, I was thinking black tie."

Theo laughed, but Tom didn't. Of the people Alex

had met so far in Alaska, Tom was the least friendly. He wondered if it was the man's nature, or if Tom had taken a sudden dislike to him. Whatever it was, Alex wasn't entirely comfortable around him.

He made his way out the door and along a winding path to his small cabin in the trees. Theo had told him he could stay out here or in the bunkhouses with the rest of the staff, and for Alex, there really was no choice.

Since his divorce, he'd come to cherish his privacy. Out here, he wouldn't disturb anyone when he couldn't sleep. Besides, he'd always dreamed of living in a cabin in the woods, and now he had the opportunity, at least for a while.

Not exactly roughing it, he mused as he opened the door and found the light switch. There was electricity and a small bathroom, but there was also a squat, fat woodstove in the corner. Alex had lit it earlier and stocked it with a good-sized log. He'd have to learn to regulate wood versus heat, because the air inside the cabin was now stifling. He left the door ajar and headed into the tiny bathroom to wash up.

Apart from the bathroom, the cabin had only one room, equipped with a rustic wooden table, two chairs and a set of bunks built into one wall. On the table, Alex had propped Annie's photo against a glass jar filled with sugar.

In one corner, a counter covered in lino and shelves holding a few dishes and a coffeepot made up a primitive kitchen. Caitlin had given him warm quilts, pillows and flannel sheets to cover the bed's blue striped mattress and thick white towels for the bathroom.

Alex showered quickly and pulled a dark sweatshirt, jeans, underwear and socks from his sports bag. He was glad he'd stopped at a Laundromat in Valdez the day before and washed his collection of dirty clothes.

As he dressed, he thought about Tom and Theo. They were both stalwart and intrinsically tough. The long, solitary drive north had demonstrated the effect environment had on people, an idea that had always intrigued him. It seemed to Alex there was a relaxed flexibility about those who lived in warmer climates. The more rugged the country became, the more it was reflected in the faces, the straightforward speech, the hardiness of its inhabitants.

Here, in the most challenging territory of all, the people he'd met were survivors, and it showed. There was an edge to them, a tough wariness. There was also an openness and sense of unity that he figured came from an awareness of the dangers of this land.

And there was often a decided risk factor in what they chose for their work—take Ivy Pierce. Being a helicopter pilot wasn't the first career choice most attractive women made.

For some reason her image was vivid in his mind, the exact shape of her face, the strange, light eyes, the delicacy of her tall frame.

In spite of that air of delicacy, he suspected she was physically strong. Her handshake was firm, and the graceful, easy way she moved indicated that her slender body was well toned. Just like her uncle and her father, Ivy had survivor written all over her.

Survival.

He reached for a thin, plastic-wrapped bundle from the side pocket of his bag and slid out four tattered letters and a worn photograph, wallet-sized and yellowed with age.

The man and woman in the picture were obviously hippies, long-haired, both wearing flared pants,loose shirts. The man was tall and rangy, and his arm was around the woman's shoulders. His face was shadowed by the wide-brimmed hat he wore, so Alex couldn't make out his features. She was pregnant, round belly poking out under the gauzy top. One of her hands rested on her belly, fingers splayed. They were laughing, squinting into the sunlight, leaning back on an old Ford.

Alex touched the man's narrow face with the tip of a finger.

You, Roy Nolan, were not a survivor. You certainly don't look like one, either. But I don't think you were a fool. So what brought you here? What were you looking for?

He'd read the letters many times over, but the answer was still elusive.

Whatever it was, Alex had come here to find it.

IVY KNOCKED at her cousin's door and, without waiting for a response, opened it, hoping to find Sage alone.

"Hey, Sage? You home?"

"Up here, Ivy." Sage's voice floated down from the second floor. Ivy trotted up the wide staircase and reached the top just as Sage burst out of a doorway down the hall, long, dark curls bouncing as she grabbed Ivy in a hug. She was shorter than Ivy, maybe five-six, with a perfect oval face and a rounded, sexy body.

"I heard the copter earlier, I was hoping you'd come over." She released Ivy and stepped back, holding both of her hands. "Another ten minutes and I'd have come looking for you, my friend." Her deep-set eyes glowed with pleasure.

"I missed you. How was your trip?" Ivy noticed the dark shadows under her friend's blue eyes, and the sadness there. "You okay, Sage?"

The nod she gave wasn't reassuring. "The trip was the usual hoopla, meeting prospective clients, doing PR, schmoozing at dinner. Ben's so much better at that than I am. It always feels phony to me." Her rich contralto voice quavered a little as she added, "And now I've got my period. Again."

"Damn. I'm really sorry, Sage." Ivy knew her friend had been trying for some time to get pregnant.

"Yeah. Me, too." She frowned. "Ben's pushing me to go to Anchorage—there's a new fertility clinic at the hospital there. But I keep hoping it'll still happen the old-fashioned way." She sounded frustrated and angry. "I keep reminding him we've only been married three years, but he insists I should've been pregnant twice by now, seeing how his first wife managed it before they were even married." She pointed at the stairs. "C'mon, let's go down and have a coffee, I just made a fresh pot. Ben's still out with those Japanese fishermen, so we've got the place to ourselves."

Ivy felt relieved that they'd have time to talk privately. "One quick coffee, I can't stay long. Dylan's taking me out for dinner."

"Aha. So have things heated up between you two?"

"Nope. Try the opposite, at least for me. He's hot, I'm not. I think I'm going to tell him tonight that he's a wonderful guy, but the chemistry just isn't right between us."

Sage led the way to the well-equipped kitchen and retrieved two mugs. "You sure of that? Maybe it'll be the sort of thing that grows over time." She poured, added a dollop of cream and handed Ivy a mug.

Ivy dropped onto a high stool by the breakfast bar. "You actually believe that's possible? That love would grow over time?"

Sage sat as well. Her wide eyes narrowed and, after a moment, she shook her head, making her thick dark curls bounce. "Not in my experience, that's for certain. I met Ben and within three seconds I was a goner."

"That's never, ever happened to me." She thought it over and amended, "Well, sexually, maybe, but emotionally, no."

"Not even with Noah?" Sage knew all about the Alaska State Trooper Ivy had come close to marrying some years ago.

"No. I *did* love Noah, but I loved flying more." She gave Sage a wry look. "I figure my wiring's screwed up. I fall in love with planes instead of people."

"Talk about safe sex." Sage giggled.

"Talk about no sex, is more like it."

"You and Dylan haven't—?"

Ivy shook her head. "Nada. He's pushing, that's why I'm opting out."

"Maybe you should give him a shot. Sometimes guys surprise you…that way."

"I'm sure he's good in the sack. He's a doctor, he's bound to know where things are and how they work. I'm just not interested. He doesn't turn me on."

"Well, from what I hear, this Tahoe Glen guy would be happy to take over. He practically salivates each time he looks at you, according to Mavis."

"God, for someone who never comes out of the

kitchen, that woman picks up on everything. Nope, no Glen, either. I'm taking a sabbatical."

"Well; I'm not. I'm ordering a couple of new nighties and some hot underwear from Victoria's Secret. Something to drive Ben wild during my fleeting fertile moments."

"You don't need nighties, Sage. You could turn guys on wearing a parka."

"Only if there was nothing underneath."

They laughed. Reluctantly, Ivy finished her coffee and got to her feet.

"Gotta go dump Dylan," she groaned.

"Wait until after dinner," Sage advised. "It's easier to do on a full stomach, and you don't want to get left with the bill if he walks out. But you don't need my advice, you're an expert at it."

"Professional dumper. Remind me to put that on my résumé." As she left, Ivy was pleased to see that Sage looked a little more cheerful.

IT WAS FUN TO JOKE with Sage about dumping guys, Ivy acknowledged on the flight back to Valdez. But it was beginning to concern her. She wasn't that far off thirty. She wanted kids as much as Sage did, although without the growing desperation she sensed in her friend.

Why didn't Ben just let up on the kid thing? He had twin daughters from a previous marriage, it wasn't as if he had no heirs. But that was Ben, he'd get something in his head and run with it until everyone wanted to throttle him. Her charismatic cousin wasn't easy to live with.

But she envied Sage the passionate relationship the two of them shared. What was it like to be a goner three minutes after meeting someone? For some reason Ivy thought of the man she'd met tonight, the guy with the Russian name.

Alex Ladrovik. Now wasn't that straight out of a spy novel? But she couldn't see him as James Bond, she decided, banking the copter for the landing at Up And Away. In spite of being a carpenter, he actually struck her more as the professor type, with his dark-rimmed glasses and that lean, intelligent face. Although he did have a kind of dark look to him, a touch mysterious. Sexy black eyes. Unruly hair, soft and golden-brown, tumbling over his forehead. Slow, deep voice, as if he thought carefully about what he was saying. And that strong jaw surely indicated a stubborn nature.

He might look like a prof, but his hands were those of a carpenter, tough and calloused, scarred and veined. No rings, she'd noticed when he hung on to her hand longer than he needed to. There'd been an awareness there, all right, certainly on his side. He'd given her the *look.*

And she'd found him interesting. But a goner? She

blew out a long breath. No goner, Ladrovik, sorry about that.

Not by a long shot.

CHAPTER SIX

You'll probably get a bundle of these letters all together, Linda, because I'm writing them from the boat, and there won't be a chance to mail anything until we reach Valdez.

From letters written by Roy Nolan,
April, 1972

BY THE END OF THE FOLLOWING week, Ivy had forgotten all about Alex Ladrovik. She hadn't quite managed to forget the devastated expression on Dylan's face, however, when she told him it was over between them. Dumping nice guys wasn't her idea of a good time, but fortunately she was far too busy to spend time feeling guilty.

Business had taken off and both she and Tom were flying their fool heads off, as he described it. Ivy had just landed a lucrative contract she'd wanted ever since they'd leased the Bell Ranger, patrolling the pipeline once a week, checking for leaks and damage. Leasing and operating the Ranger was expensive, especially now that gas prices had shot up, and this new contract went a long way toward solvency for Up And Away.

The tourist business was also booming. This morning, two Chinese businessmen and their wives had booked her for a full hour's tour, and Ivy was doing her best to make it worth their while.

"There are two bears just down to your right," she said, tilting the copter so they'd have a better view. "I'll drop down so you can take a closer look." Ivy spiraled until the furry animals were clearly visible to her customers. The bears were ambling along through a grassy meadow and looked like big lovable teddies.

"Look, there's a pair of cubs," she exclaimed. The little rascals had been hidden by a pine tree, so she hadn't spotted them right away.

"Alaska has three species of bear: brown, black and polar," she went on. "The ones you're looking at are browns. They have the greatest range, so they're the ones you're most likely to spot."

Ivy enjoyed playing professional guide, pointing out calving glaciers, tundra, snow-covered mountain peaks, hidden lakes and a huge herd of caribou. The weather had cooperated fully. It was a wonderful morning, clear skies, golden sunshine glinting off blue glaciers, only a light wind. Perfect flying weather.

The bears were a hit. Oohs and aahs and little

screams and delighted giggles sounded over her headphones, and Ivy was smiling when the call came over the radio.

She knew by the tone of Tom's voice that something was wrong.

Through the static, she heard him say, "Caitlin just radioed in an SOS. It sounds like Theo's having a heart attack. They've taken him in to Valdez Hospital, but they don't have the equipment he needs there so he has to go to Anchorage. The medevac from Anchorage is out on another call. We need the copter, stat. They'll bring him by ambulance to the pad by the office."

Adrenaline shot through Ivy's system.

"I'll be right there, ETA seven minutes."

Thank God she wasn't at the farthest point in the tour.

"There's a family emergency, we're heading back to Valdez," she told her guests. "I'll make it up to you later. Just talk to Kisha back at the office and she'll book another half hour for you, free of charge."

Six long minutes later, she hastily dumped her passengers at Up And Away. A few moments later the ambulance drove up. Medical staff hurried toward the copter, pushing her Uncle Theo on a wheeled stretcher. His face was obscured by a portable oxygen mask. With only a minimal amount of confusion, they loaded him into the back of the copter.

One of the medics climbed in beside him, and Caitlin took the seat beside Ivy. One glance at her aunt's ashen, terror-stricken face was enough to tear at Ivy's heart. She caught the wordless plea in her aunt's eyes and leaned over and kissed her.

"It's gonna be fine, Auntie Cait. We'll be at the hospital in minutes."

She ran through her takeoff routine, and then they were airborne.

Anchorage Regional Hospital was the only medical facility in the area with a landing pad for helicopters. The Valdez Hospital had radioed ahead and, as Ivy settled the Bell Ranger on the pad, emergency staff were waiting. They raced over, and within moments Theo was being whisked away, Caitlin running alongside holding his hand, the medic from Valdez bringing up the rear.

Ivy watched as they all disappeared through the wide doors. "Please," she murmured. "Please, God, help him. Please let him be okay." She realized she was trembling, and that tears were trickling down her cheeks. Finding a tissue, she blotted her eyes and blew her nose.

"Gotta get out of here," she said to nobody. Much as she longed to be with Caitlin, the medevac could be arriving at any moment and she was blocking the landing pad. Ivy debated flying out to the airport and putting the Ranger in a hangar so she could stick around, but it only took a few moments' consideration to convince her that wasn't a good idea.

There was little Ivy could do here in Anchorage, apart from giving her aunt moral support. It would be more productive to help out at the lodge. With both Caitlin and Theo absent, the full responsibility of running the place would fall on Sage and Ben. They'd need all the help available.

There were also commitments at Up And Away that couldn't be cancelled on such short notice. Guests at the lodge had booked the copter for an eagle-sighting tour that afternoon. It wasn't fair to disappoint them.

Tom was flying much-needed supplies in to remote settlements the way he did every week, and he wouldn't be able to delay his trip, either. It made better sense all round for Ivy to go straight back to Valdez.

Anchorage had wilderness at its very doorstep, and usually Ivy drank in the aerial view of mountain ranges and miles of virgin forest. But today, for the first time ever, the raw beauty of the Alaskan landscape didn't comfort her or bring her joy. She flew over it without really seeing it.

Theo and Caitlin were the very heartbeat of Raven Lodge, making the thousand and one things they did each day look easy. Ivy and Tom would pitch in, but Sage and Ben would have to take on most of the load.

Ben's twin, Logan, would undoubtedly fly in from Seattle as soon as he heard. Logan was a lawyer, and he hadn't really worked at the lodge for years, so he wouldn't know much about the routine.

There were competent guides for the fishing expeditions, but someone needed to be in charge. Ivy knew the lodge was almost fully booked. That meant eight or ten extra bodies to feed and entertain, as well as rooms to clean and laundry to do.

The bookings could be canceled, but... Her aunt would only agree in the most extreme circumstances—if—if—Ivy swallowed hard against the lump in her throat.

She couldn't think about that, so instead she concentrated on practical matters, like meals. Caitlin and Mavis did all the cooking. They had help in the summer, but right now they were on their own.

Mavis had lived at the lodge for the past fifteen years. She was eccentric, but she was an amazing cook. Because of her scarred face, however, she wouldn't serve or socialize at all with guests. Caitlin did all that. Sage could probably take over, but then there'd be no one to do the bookings and juggling of schedules.

As well as taking guests out on fishing trips, Theo kept track of their complex schedules, figuring out who was going where and when they were due back or needed to be picked up. Ben would have to take that over, or maybe it was something Logan could do.

Alex was still there, of course. Theo had planned to supervise the building of the cabins and also work along with the carpenter on their construction. Would Alex stick around?

Not likely, Ivy surmised with a sigh. After all, he was a stranger, with no investment whatsoever in the lodge. And he could easily find another carpentry job in Valdez; there was a high turnover at the hotel's construction site.

Ivy remembered to radio Tom, letting him know she was on her way back, adding that she had no idea of Theo's condition. Caitlin had promised to phone the moment there was any news, and of course Tom and Ivy could be at the hospital in about an hour with either the floatplane or the copter.

As she neared Valdez, Ivy made a decision. The only thing for her to do was to pack a bag and move out to the lodge. She hated to leave the snug little house she rented in Valdez, but there was nothing else for it. Thanks to the copter pad, she could be in Valdez in a matter of minutes to take out charter flights.

She was on the ground when she realized that the one person she hadn't even thought about in all this was Frances. Had Tom thought to call her? Probably not.

Sure, Frances kept up a facade of friendliness with

Caitlin and Theo, but Ivy knew that's all it was. A facade. Her mother never visited the lodge, even though her aunt and uncle often dropped in to see Frances and Tom when they were in Valdez.

There was no point in expecting Frances to help now, Ivy thought bitterly. It made her furious to have to admit all over again that Frances was in this family, but not of it.

LATE THAT AFTERNOON, Ivy was tossing pants and sweaters into a duffel bag in her bedroom when Tom phoned.

"Caitlin just called," he said.

"And?" Ivy's throat went dry.

"The doctors say—hold on a minute, I wrote it all down."

There was a pause, a rustle of paper, and then Tom recited, "Theo suffered a severe myocardial infarction. He isn't out of danger yet. There's been significant damage to his heart muscle, and he's going to need rest and rehabilitation. No one will say how long he might be in hospital." There was a pause and then Tom said, "Not very good news, huh?"

"No, not good." Ivy swallowed hard and stuffed underwear into a plastic bag so she'd be able to locate it easily. "But at least he's getting the best of care, Dad. Was Aunt Cait worried about the guests at the lodge?"

"Yeah, she was. I told her you were heading out,

and she was really grateful. Said to tell you it's a big relief to her, knowing you'll be there. She says Mavis isn't too good at planning menus, that maybe you could do that?"

Ivy's heart sank. She had no idea how to even go about it. How did you judge quantity? "I'll do my best," she said in a confident tone.

"Good girl."

Ivy's eyes filled with tears. It was what he'd always said when she was little. Theo's heart attack was making her aware that Tom was getting older, too.

They talked for a few moments about schedules at Up And Away, and then Tom hung up. Ivy finished packing, emptied the fridge of milk and yogurt, and was adjusting the furnace thermostat when the phone rang again.

When she answered, Frances said, "Ivy, it's me. Tom told me what's happened. He said Caitlin's concerned about the menus. If you want to do them, that's absolutely fine, but if you don't have time, I'd enjoy working them out. I could put them on the computer at school each day and then e-mail them to Sage. It would be best not to tell Mavis I'm doing them, though. I suspect she's rather territorial when it comes to the kitchen. What do you think?"

It was a huge relief. "Great idea, Mom."

"That's settled, then. Let me know if there's anything else I can do."

She'd misjudged her mother, Ivy realized when the call ended. But all she had to go on was the past. And Frances didn't really have much of a track record there, did she?

Ivy soon learned Frances was right about Mavis. The eccentric little woman was not a happy camper with Caitlin absent. She resented any change in her routine. She was much more cantankerous and stubborn than Ivy had suspected she'd be, and she made it plain she wasn't happy about taking direction from either Sage or Ivy. She argued with them over everything and bossed them mercilessly.

By the third evening, Ivy had learned the hard way what a mad scramble it was to feed eight guests and a varying number of employees three times a day. Neighbors had learned of Theo's illness and were beginning to send food. Ivy and Sage welcomed all donations with grateful hearts and profuse thanks. Mavis, on the other hand, resented the offerings. "They figure I can't manage on my own?" she snorted each time a casserole or some baking appeared. "They figure I'm over the hill?"

Ivy tried to calm her down by saying—truthfully—that she couldn't imagine how Caitlin and Mavis did it, week in and week out, all during the season. And the dishes. There was a dishwasher, but it ran off the generator, and if guests were showering it took forever to put a load through.

"You young folks can do the hand washing," Mavis proclaimed the very first night, as if she was granting a gift, and as soon as dinner was served, she disappeared up the back stairs to her room. Ivy figured the older woman was probably exhausted and too proud to admit it. Lord knows *she* was exhausted, and she was only half Mavis's age.

Tonight, Sage was busy changing linens in the guest bedrooms for a new group arriving in the morning, so Ivy was on her own with a mountain of pots and pans. She was grateful when Alex appeared beside her. He gently shoved her aside and rolled up the sleeves of his sweatshirt.

"You dry. My hands could use a good soak in hot water," he said, handing her a tea towel. "I got grease on them from that motor Oliver and I were trying to repair."

"Did you get it fixed?" During the past several days, Ivy'd been impressed by Alex. Instead of heading back to Valdez as she'd expected, he'd stayed on, quietly and efficiently taking on whatever needed doing, from working in the kitchen to waiting tables to helping clean the boats and outfit them for the next day's excursion. He was cheerful, and he seemed to have a sixth sense as to where he was needed.

"Oliver thinks we did. I'm not so confident. Motors aren't my area of expertise." He carefully washed a pot, handed it to Ivy to dry and reached for another, his motions efficient and methodical. They worked in silence for a few moments.

Ivy studied his hands. He had long fingers, calloused. And yet somehow his hands seemed refined, a workman's hands but with class. That's what this guy was, she decided, drying another casserole dish. Alex was classy blue collar.

His voice snapped her out of her reverie. "That chicken stuff was fantastic, but this pan it baked in doesn't want to come clean." He reached for a plastic scrubber and rubbed hard.

"A friend of Caitlin's, Mary Louise Bell, sent that over," Ivy said. "She runs Bell House, a B&B a few miles out of Valdez."

"Nice folks, bringing food. It's a lot different here than it is in the city," he remarked. "Two guys came by today in a boat, offered to help me dig the foundation for the cabins."

Ivy nodded. "Alaskans are like that, really neighborly."

"I've noticed." Alex rinsed the pan and handed it to her. "I have a theory that it's the climate. You know, man against nature."

He was studying her face as if he intended to memorize every feature. Ivy rubbed at a damp spot on the casserole dish and tried to ignore his gaze.

"That and the fact that there aren't many people in the state. 640,000, latest census." How could you feel sexy about a man up to his elbows in soapsuds? But she did. "Even though where area is concerned," she babbled, "we're one fifth the size of the entire U.S.A."

God, when had she started sounding like a schoolteacher—and a dull one at that?

"Spoken like a tour guide," he said. He had a dimple in one cheek when he smiled. The steam was fogging up his glasses, and he wiped at them with his shirtsleeve.

"Well, you have to know those things, if you're going to fly tourists around," she defended herself. "Just like Aunt Caitlin has to know how to plan meals for dozens of people, and use what's available because she can't always get to a store."

"Your aunt's an amazing woman," Alex agreed, turning back to the sink. "And your uncle's no slouch, either. Not that I had time to really get to know them." He scrubbed out a lasagna pan, rinsed it and handed it to Ivy.

Their fingers touched. His were wet and he had dark hair on the backs of his wrists. He was giving her that look again, heavy-lidded, a sexy look that had nothing to do with Theo and Cait, or pots, either.

"I need a dry towel," she said, opening a drawer, giving herself time to calm down. "Uncle Theo's always spoiled me," she said, trying to sound casual. "Some of my best recipes have come from Aunt

Caitlin. I keep telling her she needs to write a cookbook. Everyone who stays here would buy one."

"You like to cook, Ivy?"

She smiled back at him this time. "Next to flying, it's my favorite thing. And then eating comes third. When I was little, Dad would fly me up here and I'd stay for a sleepover. No matter how busy she was, Caitlin would always take time to teach me how to make cookies or scones. She makes the best scones."

He was scrubbing a frying pan now. "Theo told me how long his family's lived here. He didn't say where they came from. Were they part of the gold rush?"

"Yeah, they were." Ivy leaned against the counter, partly because she was feeling tired—it had been an exceptionally long and hectic day—but mostly so she could watch his face while they talked. There was something about Alex's face that she found intriguing. He didn't smile much, but when he did it was worth waiting for.

She forced herself to stop staring. "You want the long Galloway history, or the short?"

He wiped his forehead with a wet hand. "Make it the long one. We still have a ways to go with these damn pots."

"Okay." She thought for a moment, organizing what she knew. "Theo's grandfather, William Galloway, emigrated from Scotland just when the Alaska gold rush started, 1896, thereabouts. William's twin brother, Robert, came with him from Edinburgh, and they got caught up in the excitement."

"Gold fever," Alex drawled.

"You got it. Instead of getting jobs building the Canadian railway the way they'd planned, they headed for the Klondike, taking William's wife, Jenny, along. That's her and William above the fireplace in the living room."

"Lovely lady. Like you, Ivy."

"Idiot." She flicked the tea towel at his butt. Nice-shaped butt, she noted. "I'm not even related, except by marriage."

"Of course not." He looked at her, and she could see the admiration in his eyes. "I didn't say you looked like her. I simply meant that both of you are beautiful."

"You need new glasses." She hated when men said that, because she knew it wasn't true. She knew what female beauty looked like, and she wasn't close. Attractive, maybe. Beautiful, no.

"Anyway," she went on, "they spent some time prospecting in Dawson, but they didn't strike it rich. William was an engineer by trade, and he gave up on gold and started thinking transportation, which was a smart move. He was one of the driving forces behind the building of the White Pass and Yukon Railway."

Alex had stopped scrubbing and was watching her. "I read about that railway before I came north. Quite an engineering feat."

"Keep going, we're almost done." She nodded toward the frying pan and iron soup pot that still needed washing. "It's mostly used to transport tourists now, but it brought thousands of prospectors and their supplies to the Klondike Gold Rush. Anyhow, there was some kind of family quarrel that resulted in Robert immigrating to Australia, and when the gold thing didn't work for them, William and Jenny left Dawson and came here to Prince William Sound, because they'd fallen in love with Alaska."

"Got bitten by the ice worm?" Alex said.

"There actually are ice worms, you know. They eat snow algae and pollen, and somehow they bore their way deep into the glaciers."

He let the greasy water out of the sink. "*You* ought to write a book, Ms. Pierce. Ice worms and other little-known facts about Alaska."

It was hard to stay focused. He had wonderful arms and shoulders, slender but still muscular.

"William and Jenny moved to Prince William Sound," Alex prompted, refilling the sink with fresh hot water and adding dish soap.

"William was an entrepreneur, and when he got here he saw the potential for a salmon packing plant, which he designed and had built. It was madly successful and, under his guidance, it grew into a complete, self-sufficient community, with its own store and post office, relying on carrier pigeons for communicating anything urgent."

"Carrier pigeons?" He laughed. "You're making this up, Pierce."

He had a great laugh, rich and free. Too bad he didn't laugh more.

"Not a word of it. William built Jenny this house." Ivy dried another pot and stowed it away. "She started having babies to fill it, a son named Bruce, and twin daughters, Martha and Emma."

"So William built the family homestead to accommodate them." He scrubbed hard at yet another encrusted pan. "His buildings were intended to last. The workmanship on this lodge is amazing."

"It's been upgraded and added on to, but basically it's still Jenny's house." She studied his face from the side. Good jaw, great mouth. "The white clapboard bunkhouse where the guides are staying was originally lodging for the single cannery workers."

"And the cabins we have?"

So he'd noticed she'd moved in not far from him. "For the married help. And the supervisors."

"Supervisors must have had much lower expectations in those days. So the Galloway kids stayed here and carried on the family business?"

"Their son, Bruce did. Theo's father. And one of William's daughters, Martha, lived here as well. Theo's aunt, I remember her, she was an old lady when I was little. Apparently Emma died when she was young. I think she's buried in the old graveyard up on the hill. I know Martha is."

He tackled the last frying pan. "So when did it stop being a cannery?"

"After Alaska became a state in 1959. There were severe regulations imposed at that time that made the salmon harvest too unpredictable."

He rinsed the pan and set it on the range to finish drying. "Trust government to screw up a good thing."

"Aah, a cynic. You'll fit right in up here." For however long you stick around. "Well, Theo didn't want to leave, so he gradually converted the cannery to a fishing lodge. Business was slow at first, but it's gradually gotten more and more popular. Aunt Caitlin's cooking helped a lot. They're now getting bookings a year ahead."

"And I think we're finally finished the dishes." He emptied the sink a second time and wrung out the cloth, folding it neatly on the drain board. "I now have the cleanest hands in all of Valdez." He held them up for her to inspect.

"That'll earn you a gold star." Ivy tossed the towel away. "I'm totally sick of drying pots. I'm going to have a cup of tea and then go to bed."

"Mind if I join you?"

Ivy quickly looked over at him, one hand on the tea canister. Did he have any idea what he'd just said? From the innocent expression on his face, she guessed he didn't. She cleared her throat and pulled out two tea bags. "Not at all. Herbal okay?"

"I'm easy."

This time she had to bite her lip to stop from laughing. He just shoved his glasses up farther on his nose.

She liked watching him do that. She liked him. More than liked. She was powerfully attracted to him. Ivy found the teapot and dropped the chamomile in while he plugged in the kettle. To heck with warming the pot. Why couldn't she have felt this way about Dylan? But no, for her libido to kick in big time she had to choose a tourist who'd be here today, gone tomorrow.

She watched him hanging the pots on the rack above the table. He had this long, strong body. He was decorative all right, definitely easy on the eyes.

He poured them each a mug of tea and slid into a chair beside hers.

"So what brings you to Alaska, Alex?" She stirred honey into her mug and offered the sticky jar to him, but he shook his head.

He didn't answer right away. Instead, he sipped at his tea. His evasiveness suddenly reminded her of Frances.

"Forget I asked," she snapped. "It's none of my business anyway."

"I was wondering where to start, is all." His

surprise showed in his voice. "See, I divorced three years ago, changed jobs, went through a sort of assessment process to figure out which direction I wanted to go. What I wanted to be when I grew up," he said in a wry tone. "I guess this trip is still part of that process."

Ivy sorted that information and then decided to run with what seemed the least invasive question. "What did you do before you became a carpenter?"

"Forensic consultant for the San Diego police department. I have a degree in anthropology."

CHAPTER SEVEN

I keep waiting to see the Northern Lights. Everybody talks about them, but they've yet to make an appearance. Probably not far enough north just yet, this old tub doesn't exactly break any speed limits.

From letters written by Roy Nolan,
April, 1972

IVY KEPT HER JAW from dropping, but only barely.

"You have a degree in anthropology, and you decided to become a carpenter?" She was trying to get her mind around it, busy reshuffling the cards she'd dealt him. Served her right for having preconceived notions.

"Lateral move," he said with a wink.

"Well, you sure fit right in up here. We all seem to be taking the road less traveled."

"I've noticed."

"You think you'll stick with a hammer?"

He took a long time to answer that, as well. This time she was more patient. She was getting used to his deliberate manner.

"No," he finally said. "I suspect I'll be heading home when the summer's over. I wasn't actually planning to be a carpenter for the rest of my life. It started out as an interim thing."

"How so?"

"A friend of mine from high school had a construction company and he was short a carpenter. I've always worked with wood in my spare time. My hobby was restoring furniture, remodeling houses. It was a good fit. Then his contract ended, and I was sort of at loose ends, so I came up here."

"Just on the spur of the moment?" There seemed to be huge gaps in this story.

"Yeah, pretty much." He shrugged his shoulders. "Everybody wants to visit Alaska these days. It's the new Aruba."

Ivy laughed. "We can only hope. Maybe this tourism boom will be more stable than furs, or gold or oil." She yawned so hard her eyes watered and her jaw cracked. "Excuse me. Long day. Must get to bed." She drained her mug and got to her feet.

"C'mon, I'll walk you to your cabin."

"It's a pretty long walk. You sure you're up for it?" They both knew that he had to pass her cabin to reach his own anyway.

"For you, fair lady, anything."

Outside it was still twilight, even though it was past ten.

The temperature had dropped. Ivy tipped her head back and then caught her breath. "Look." She pointed up at the sky where a soft, mysterious glow stretched in a wide band. It began to flicker, fading in and out, taking on color in shimmering green, pink, white.

"Aurora borealis," she whispered. There were no words to capture the magnificence that filled the sky like paint on a giant canvas. No, not a static painting. Bright yellow-green melded with purple, blue, red and deeper green, into a celestial kaleidoscope.

Ivy knew she ought to go and alert the guests. This sort of extravagant display wasn't usual, even for Alaska. But she couldn't force herself to move.

She had no idea how long they stood there, transfixed, silent. Alex fumbled for her hand, lacing her fingers with his, linking palm to palm. When at last the glow faded, disappearing a little at a time until the night sky took on its usual star-studded appearance, Ivy shivered and remembered to breathe again.

She heard Alex also draw a shuddering breath. Still holding her hand, he walked beside her along the path to the cabins, not saying a word, and gratitude filled her.

She hated having someone explain the scientific facts surrounding the northern lights, the sunspots and solar flares that ionize particles in the upper atmosphere. In her mind, the only suitable acknowledgment was silence. Reverence.

At the door to her cabin his hand tightened on hers momentarily and then he released his grip and took a step back.

"Night, Ivy. Sleep well," he said quietly.

"You, too." She went inside and closed the door, and a few moments later heard the door to his cabin close as well.

You're a rare one, Alex, she decided as she showered and collapsed onto the hard mattress on the lower bunk.

Usually, men were drawn to her more than she was to them. With Alex, the pattern may have reversed itself, and it was unsettling. It was also fun. With a weary grin, she curled on her side and began to slide into sleep.

She'd never believed that there was one special someone out there, waiting for her to find him. Or vice versa. She'd decided long ago that, with a few rare exceptions, people usually settled for whoever was available when the nesting instinct kicked in.

Now, however, she wasn't quite so certain.

TWO DAYS LATER, Alex wiped away the sweat rolling down his forehead and leaned on his shovel, surveying the sizeable hole he'd already excavated that morning. He still had one hell of a way to go, but he wanted to show the guys who were arriving this afternoon to help that he wasn't some slackass from the lower forty-eight.

Theo had told him that the foundation for the cabins had to be fifty-four inches deep to protect against frost heaves. That was some righteous pile of dirt to move by hand, even for three men. His sweaty black T-shirt was stuck to his back, so he pulled it off, using it to clean the perspiration off his glasses before he tossed it toward the flannel shirt he'd discarded an hour ago. Then he dug the shovel into the gravel again and heaved it up and out, finding the rhythm and enjoying it.

Nothing like a challenge to keep your mind occupied. Nothing like shoveling to keep your muscles hard and tire you out so maybe you'd sleep more than three hours at night.

"Hey, earth mover. Ready for a coffee break?" Ivy stood on the pile of dirt, smiling down at him. Her cheeks were flushed, and for a moment he had the feeling she might have been ogling his bare back, but that was probably his ego talking. She had a red thermos in one hand, cups and a covered plastic container in the other.

"Yes, ma'am," he said fervently, stepping out of the hole.

"Let's take it over to the picnic bench," she said,

motioning to a rustic wooden bench under a birch tree. He caught her shooting a furtive fast glance at his bare chest.

She covered herself by saying, “You might want your shirt, Professor. It’s chilly in the shade.”

He grabbed it, tugging it over his head as she walked ahead of him. He couldn’t help but admire the view. Her worn jeans fit like a second skin, outlining her round bottom, narrowing to a handspan waist. He imagined cupping that lovely ass in his palms, and then forced himself to drag his eyes away and center his attention higher up, on her slender neck, the way her bright hair curled madly all over her skull.

It was a relief to swing his legs over the bench and sit down.

“I have cookies as well as coffee,” she said, filling two cups and adding sugar and powdered cream to both. “Sorry—couldn’t carry real cream. Hope you don’t mind.” That she even remembered he took it pleased him.

She held out the container. “These are Auntie’s famous peanut butter oatmeal chocolate chip bombs. So called because they give you what Mavis calls The Wind. But they’re worth it.”

He laughed as he reached for one. “I’ll take my chances.” He finished off the cookie in two bites, giving an appreciative grunt as he washed it all down with a gulp of coffee. “This is kind of you. Thanks, Ivy.”

"Not so kind as all that. I really needed to get out of that kitchen." She rolled her eyes. "Mavis is on a tear about the way Sage and I did the breakfasts this morning. Apparently there's a system and we botched it by letting guests pour their own juice and make their own toast. Mavis was scandalized. As penance I've been peeling vegetables—we're making shepherd's pie for supper. Man, are we making shepherd's pie! There's enough to feed the military. My fingers are permanently crippled."

"What happened to Mavis?"

"A pressure cooker blew up. I never knew her any other way, so I don't even notice her scars."

"She could probably have plastic surgery."

Ivy shook her head. "A couple years ago one of the guests—a doctor—suggested it to her. She told him to go to hell."

"She's one tough lady." He washed down another mouthful of cookie with coffee. "Has she got you chained to the paring knife the rest of the day?"

"Thank God I have a job that gets me away from Mavis, otherwise there'd be bloodshed. I have to take the copter into Valdez in half an hour. There's a group of tourists who want to go up at the same time and they won't all fit in the floatplane."

He couldn't say it sounded like fun, because it was his worst nightmare. "When did you learn to fly, Ivy?"

"Oh, Captain used to take me up when I could barely walk."

Her face lit up whenever she mentioned Tom. Alex also remembered the smile on Tom's face when Ivy was around. Father and daughter shared a powerful bond, no doubt about it. He felt a stab of pain, realizing what he'd lost with Annie. And also, what he'd never had as a boy. His relationship with Steve Ladrovik had been powerful, but it sure as hell hadn't been positive.

"When I was about seven," Ivy was saying, "Dad started letting me sit on his lap and steer. By the time I was ten, I was landing the floatplane by myself."

"Ten, huh?" Just talking about landing a floatplane made him queasy. "And let me guess, by twelve you were piloting the helicopter?"

She laughed. "Not quite. But that was Dad, again. He knew how to fly copters—flew them in Vietnam. He showed me the basics, and then I went to flight school in Anchorage, got my accreditation. Right now we lease that baby—" she gestured at the helicopter on its cement pad "—but we're saving up to buy one of our own." She drank some of her coffee. "I'll take you up sometime, if you want. Do you like to fly?"

"Not much, but I've only ever flown on commercial flights." And gotten airsick every time. "I can't say I really liked it. More necessity than pleasure."

"Commercial flights." She blew out a derogatory breath. "That's not really flying, that's just transportation. You've got to go up in a small craft on a blue-sky day in Alaska to really appreciate flying." She glanced at her watch. "I'd take you today, except I'm booked."

He thanked God for small blessings.

"I should get going."

And he should get back to work. Except... "Have you ever been married, Ivy?" Now where the hell had that come from? "Sorry, I didn't mean to get so personal."

"That's okay, how else do we get to know one another? And the answer's no, no wedding album in my bookcase."

He waited, and she laughed. "Okay, I came close once," she confessed. "But I realized in time that I wasn't ready to settle down. We're still friends. He married a woman from town and moved to Portland. They've got two kids already." She gave him a long, considering look. "My turn at personal—this *is* a democracy, Professor. So, where did you grow up, what did your father do, how many kids are in your family?"

"Not fair, that's three in one."

"Economy. Answer fast, I have to go." Her grin was cocky. He had the urge to lean across the table and kiss the mischief off her mouth.

"Threats, huh? Okay, San Diego, aeronautical engineer and there are three of us. I'm oldest, then Zelda, then Dmitri." He added without planning to, "Steve Ladrovik was my stepfather, so Zelda and

Dmitri are my half siblings." He was still getting used to that himself.

He saw her mulling it over and to fend off questions that could turn awkward he said the first thing that came into his head. "My turn, you owe me two. How old are you, Ivy?"

"Twenty-seven. I'll be twenty-eight July 19th. How about you?"

"Thirty-four, almost thirty-five." Seven years and untold chasms of living between them.

"When's your birthday?"

"May 6th."

"Wow, just a few weeks away. Tell you what, I'll take you up for a birthday ride."

When he didn't respond she added quickly, "If you're still around, that is." She looked at her watch again. "Gotta fly. Literally." She slid her long legs out from under the picnic table. "Don't strain yourself with that shovel."

"Be careful up there." Alex watched her stride toward the helicopter. She walked as if she owned the earth. When the rotors began to whir, he felt nervous for her. It wasn't until the grotesque bird had lifted, circled and then disappeared over the mountain that he got up and headed back to the hole, digging the shovel in and heaving it up and out, finding his rhythm again. *Trying not to think about Ivy.*

He'd had two casual sexual encounters since his

divorce, and both had left him so empty inside he'd decided not to go that route again.

This might explain this ache in his groin whenever he was around Ivy. He was a man, she was a sensual woman. Different physical type from Rebecca, which was probably a good thing.

His ex-wife was tiny and softly rounded, with long, silky dark hair. Sage Galloway actually reminded him of her.

His *former* wife, Rebecca had suggested he call her, last time they'd talked. It sounded more civilized than ex, she'd said with that captivating gamine grin.

Rebecca's smile had stolen his heart the first time they'd met. It had been outside a courtroom where he was presenting forensic evidence for the defense and she was the cop appearing as a witness for the prosecution.

Rebecca hadn't fit his idea of what a cop looked like.

She wasn't on the force anymore. After Annie died, she'd taken a leave of absence and never went back. Now she was a grief counselor with parents who'd lost children.

They'd met for coffee at a Starbucks just before he left San Diego for Alaska. He'd wanted to tell her about Steve's death and show her the letters and the photo his mother had given him. Rebecca was fond of Linda; they still talked on the phone every couple weeks.

His mother's revelation had been a tremendous shock, and he'd needed to talk to someone who knew him, knew his history. Rebecca had known him better than anyone else. Telling her was easier than he'd expected, because she listened the way she always had, attentive and quiet, sipping her soy latte, nodding now and then.

When he was done, she'd said, "So now you feel you have to find out who your real father was. Well, I can understand that. But do you have to go to Alaska for that? You could trace his family on the Net, maybe find relatives in Canada. Why Alaska?"

He'd asked himself the same question, but the answer had escaped him. It still did. "He died up there, I'd like to find out why, if I can." That answer had seemed unsatisfactory when he said it to Rebecca at the time, but it was all he could articulate—even now. And he rejected her suggestion that he was running away…from what happened to Annie.

She, more than anyone, must know that Annie was a part of him, that she went wherever he was. That her memory would be with him no matter where he ended up.

And when Rebecca told him about her friend—a man who'd lost his son—Alex had felt only relief. He sincerely wanted her to be happy.

He told her so, and she took his hand and linked her fingers through his, the way she'd always done.

The way he'd done the other night with Ivy.

"Find someone to love, Alex. Start over." She'd smiled at him. "Annie would want us *both* to be happy."

The memory infuriated him, just as her words had that afternoon, and he drove the spade into the earth with savage force.

Rebecca might, but he couldn't, *wouldn't,* ever go to that illusory place he'd inhabited with Rebecca again. Where he'd trusted that the people he loved lived happily ever after and healthy little girls didn't die.

Start over, find someone to love? If that kind of simplistic pop psychology worked for Rebecca, great. But there was no way in hell he'd ever take that big a chance again. Because he knew he'd never survive if he lost his heart a second time.

Which was why it would make good sense to keep his distance from Ivy Pierce.

CHAPTER EIGHT

There's a couple other guys on this boat, heading north like I am because it's something they've always dreamed of doing. They're climbers heading for a mountain called The Devil's Thumb. Climbing's always seemed way too dangerous to me. I don't even like elevators much.

From letters written by Roy Nolan,
April, 1972

INSTEAD OF KEEPING his distance from Ivy, Alex ended up sitting far too close to her—at 6:30 the following morning, in the damned helicopter.

As the rotors whirled, Ivy did something complicated with knobs and sticks and the copter rose as fast as Alex's stomach dropped. In sickening seconds they were high above the lodge, tipping to the right, straightening, and then heading at what felt like ten miles an hour toward Valdez and the dentist. Except Alex knew they were doing over a hundred—he could see the gauge.

He fought to keep from heaving up the banana bread that had caused this calamity. He'd been eating a thick slice with his morning coffee an hour before when he crunched into a walnut shell and felt the filling drop out of his right upper molar. The immediate jolt from the hot coffee convinced him if a dentist was available, he was a candidate.

He made the mistake of saying so. Ivy just happened to be heading for Valdez in the copter. How could he refuse to go with her without revealing he was a sniveling coward?

He swallowed the bile rising in his throat, and Ivy gestured at the headset. He slipped it on.

"Couldn't wait until your birthday for a ride, huh, Professor?" she said cheerfully. "Too bad about your tooth, but Doc Banyen's the best, he'll fix it for you in no time. So just relax and enjoy the ride. And try to keep your tongue out of the cavity." She pointed out at the Sound. "Good view of Columbia Glacier from up here, it's great that the sun's out and the weather's fine. It's not so much fun on a rainy day."

Fun was the last word he'd have used. A fast, horrifying glimpse confirmed that the panoramic view probably *was* spectacular. Alex was too terrified to appreciate it. The earth was far below and dropping, and all that kept him from hurtling down to meet it was the fragile Plexiglas floor beneath his quaking boots.

He concentrated instead on Ivy's long leg, inches from his own, her long fingers on the steering mechanism. He noted her easy, practiced grace as she maneuvered the copter, the relaxed smile on her lips as she pointed out things he should look at.

This was her world. It showed in the lilt in her husky tone, the wide grin she shot him when a sudden change in altitude made him cry out and grab for a handhold.

It was her world, and there was no way it would ever be his. He needed to remember this the next time he lusted after her.

He felt a surge of relief as the landing pad near Valdez came into view and prayed fervently as they descended. The machine hovered before settling with hardly a bump.

Alex realized he'd been holding his breath. It took a moment for him to unclench his grip on the safety bar.

When the noise died and the rotors slowed, Ivy said, "So, Professor, you ready for flying lessons?"

"Not in this lifetime."

"It grows on you." She laughed, unbuckling her safety belt, gesturing at the door. "I'll drive you into town and introduce you to Harold. My guests aren't due for another forty minutes. But first come meet Bert and Kisha. He's our resident mechanic, she answers the phone and the radio and keeps the accounts in order for us. Dad and I are hopeless when it comes to bookkeeping. Bert's also a student pilot—Dad's teaching him to fly the Beaver."

She led the way into the mobile unit. A stocky young man with a brush cut was sitting in front of a desk while a round little woman tapped away at the keys of a computer terminal. The man got to his feet and nodded at Ivy.

"Kisha Harris, this is Alex Ladrovik," she said.

"How do you do, Kisha?" Alex liked the way her eyes crinkled and her cheeks bunched when she smiled.

"Bert Ambrose, this is my friend Alex Ladrovik," Ivy said next, spelling out Alex's name on her fingers, alerting Alex to the fact that Bert was deaf.

Bert stuck his hand out to Alex. "Good to meet you," he said, slurring the words into one.

"I know some sign, little bit." Alex matched the spoken words with the ASL equivalent, and Bert's eyebrows shot up. Alex measured out a scant inch between thumb and forefinger. "About that much."

Bert's fingers flew. "How did you learn?"

Alex's fingers felt stiff and clumsy. "My girlfriend in high school had deaf parents. She taught me." He hadn't used sign in a long while, but he found it was coming back to him.

"My girlfriend is hearing," Bert signed, gesturing toward Kisha, who blushed and rolled her eyes. "She teaches me voice words."

"The things a guy will do for a pretty woman," Alex signed, and Bert laughed and agreed.

Ivy had only heard Alex's side of the conversation, and she made a questioning gesture. "You guys are going way too fast for me to follow. What's funny?"

Alex explained.

Ivy snorted. Kisha said, *"Men,"* and went back to the computer.

Bert's fingers were flying again. "Good to meet someone who knows sign. Maybe we have a beer some evening?"

Alex hesitated. "I'd like that, but I'm working out at Raven Lodge, so I'd have to hitch a ride in with Ivy or borrow a boat."

"No problem, I could come with boat and get you. Soon I have license, then I bring floatplane, pick you up."

"Thanks." Alex hoped the apprehension he felt didn't show on his face. The only thing more nerve-wracking than being taxied around in a helicopter would be flying in a floatplane with a beginner pilot. He hesitated and then signed, "Planes scare the shit out of me, but I haven't told Ivy yet. I'm trying to be macho."

Bert laughed for a long time. "My dad has boat, I'll come pick you up with that."

"Thank you."

Ivy had been watching their exchange with a

bemused expression. "Sorry to break this up, guys, but I'd better get Alex to the dentist so I can keep my date with the tourists."

"Broke my tooth this morning," Alex explained to Bert.

"Hate dentists," Bert signed vehemently.

"Me, too. Almost as much as flying."

They left Bert guffawing over that one. When they were outside, Ivy gave him an assessing glance. "So, an anthropologist who worked as a forensic scientist and retired to become a carpenter also knows sign language. You're a regular Renaissance man, Ladrovik."

"Right now I'm a desperate man." The cool air was sending bolts of pain through the nerves in his broken tooth. "Damn it, I don't do pain at all well." He clamped a hand over his mouth.

She was grinning at him. "Most guys don't. Which is why God chose women for childbirth." She opened the passenger door on a fire-engine-red truck and he climbed in.

To say Ivy was a fast driver was like comparing Columbia Glacier to an ice cube. Alex didn't allow himself to clutch at the armrest as they tore around corners and roared down blessedly quiet streets—it was a truck, after all, not a helicopter—but he was tempted. By the time she pulled into a parking spot in front of a medical building on Meals Avenue, his teeth were clenched as if he had lockjaw, which wasn't helping the aching tooth at all.

Ivy didn't seem to notice. "I'll come in and introduce you."

The office was definitely casual. There were kids' drawings up on the bulletin board and a receptionist's desk, but no one was there. Ivy sailed past it, sticking her head into a treatment room.

Alex, who was waiting in the reception area, heard her say, "Hey, Harry, how you doing, buddy? I've got a customer for you."

"And here I thought you were here because you'd changed your mind about marrying me," a bass voice replied. "I'll be right out, Ivy."

The handsome man who appeared a moment later could easily have qualified for professional football. Alex estimated him at six-five, two-eighty, and all of it muscle. His shoulders barely made it through the door. He was wearing a plain white T-shirt and jeans, and his wide smile was either an advertisement for his job or the best set of porcelain veneers Alex had ever seen.

Ivy introduced them, and Alex felt irritated by the familiar way Harry slung an arm around Ivy's shoulders. Did he have to flaunt his attraction?

Alex explained what had happened to his tooth, adding, "I don't have an appointment, do you think you can fit me in?"

"Any friend of Ivy's gets special treatment around here. Sit down, I'll finish up with Billy and then I'll take a look."

"Gotta go," Ivy said. "Thanks, Harry." She turned to Alex. "I won't be heading back to the lodge till late afternoon. If you need to get back before that you can probably hitch a boat ride with someone. There's always a fisherman or guide heading up the Sound."

"I'll probably do that." He'd swim if it meant avoiding another ride in that helicopter. "Thanks, Ivy."

Harry disappeared back into the treatment room, and Alex sat down. Maybe he'd take advantage of being in Valdez. Today was a good time to visit the police office. He had the official letter they'd sent his mother two years after Roy Nolan went missing, telling her they'd recovered his knapsack and assumed he was dead, although his body had never been found. For some reason they'd kept the knapsack, maybe because Linda had never requested it. He'd go claim it if it was still around, Alex decided, thumbing through a copy of *National Geographic.*

It wasn't long before Billy, who looked seventeen and still seemed to be in acute pain, staggered out, grabbed his jacket and made a break for freedom.

Harry ushered Alex into the cubicle.

"Let's have a look here. Yup, I see the problem all right, got a real crevasse there. I'll get that filled for you in no time." He began laying out a tray. "You're staying at the lodge, Ivy said. Skiing?"

"No." Now his tooth was sending pain right down his neck, and he didn't feel much like talking.

Harry obviously did. "So how's Theo doing? Terrible about his heart."

Alex wished to God the dentist would just get on with it. "He's recovering, but it's taking time. No word yet on how long he'll be in hospital."

"He's a great guy, Theo. Is Logan still around? I heard he flew in when Theo had the heart attack."

It took Alex a moment to figure out Harry was referring to Ben's twin brother. "He's gone back to Seattle. I didn't meet him—he stayed in Anchorage until Theo was out of danger."

"Didn't come home at all, huh? Figures. Word on the street is him and Ben don't get along too well. Brothers, what can I say? I never got along with mine, either. Still don't. He's homophobic as hell."

Alex digested the implications of that bit of surprising information.

"Is that a problem up here? Valdez does seem a little more redneck than say, San Francisco."

Harry laughed as he picked up the syringe.

"That's where we lived before my partner got a job here at the refinery. He's an engineer. A guy will do the damnedest things for love. I miss San Fran like crazy. Okay, let's get this molar repaired. You want to take your glasses off? Good, thanks. Now lie back and relax, you won't feel a thing."

Harry was an optimist, but he was also good with a needle. The freezing went in painlessly, and while the huge man rooted around his mouth, Alex thought about his own brother.

Dmitri was six years younger and, when he was small, he'd driven Alex nuts by tagging along with him everywhere. But as Dmitri grew, it soon became clear that he was the son Steve Ladrovik wanted Alex to be.

Dmitri was outgoing, a natural athlete who shared his father's love for team sports. Alex was a loner. His preferred activity was long-distance running, and he had no interest in competing in or even watching sports.

Too bad he hadn't known when he was growing up that he wasn't related by blood to his father. The truth might've made it easier to get along with Steve. He might've been a better brother to Dmitri.

"There we go, good as new. You have another couple fillings that need replacing. If you want me to do them, just say the word, I'll book you in."

Alex's lip was frozen and he tried not to lisp. "Thanks, but I won't be around long enough."

"Just passing through, huh? Well, enjoy your stay. Get those teeth looked at when you get home." Harry clapped him on the back and took his charge card. After Alex signed the slip, he hurried out.

He made a stop at the drugstore and asked the clerk for directions. She told him that the police station was inside city hall on Chenega Avenue, right in the heart of downtown Valdez. With his mouth now solidly frozen, Alex made his way to the reception desk. A young woman in a low-cut green blouse raised her eyebrows at him.

"I'd like to talk to someone about an old file concerning a missing person," Alex said, trying to speak clearly. He hoped he wasn't drooling.

"That would be Officer Wahlbergh. Sit down and I'll let him know you're here."

Moments later, a balding, portly policeman with worry lines etched into his forehead led Alex into a small office.

"What can I do for you, Mr. Ladrovik?"

It was hard to know where to begin. The freezing in his mouth made him opt for the short version.

"My father disappeared north of Valdez, in the spring of 1972. His name was Roy Nolan. He walked into the bush and was never heard from again. His body was never found. I'd like to see any files you might have on him. His knapsack was located that fall, and I'd like to claim it if it's still around."

He showed Wahlbergh the copy of his original birth certificate, naming him as Jack Nolan and his father as Roy Nolan.

He also had his adoptive one, giving the name

Steve Ladrovik had chosen for him. Until Steve's death, Alex hadn't known he'd started out as Jack. Linda had told him Nolan named him for Jack London, his favorite writer. He'd briefly considered exchanging Alex for Jack, but it didn't feel comfortable. And what was the point?

Wahlbergh studied both documents carefully and also asked for a driver's license, which Alex produced.

"The file should be stored down the hall in dead records," Wahlbergh said. "Sit tight, I'll see if I can locate it. And the knapsack might be in the evidence locker, although it's pretty unlikely it's still around. Don't know why they wouldn't have sent it on to your mother."

Alex waited for what felt like a very long time. His jaw ached as the freezing began to subside.

"You're in luck, young man." Wahlbergh set a dusty cardboard carton on the desk and lifted the lid. "The knapsack's here all right. And I found the file as well." He laid a slim manila folder beside the box. "Turns out the investigating officer on that case was a friend of my old man, Johnny Kusak. Good cop, Johnny. Unfortunately, he's been dead for five years. Might have been nice to talk to him."

"Could I have a copy of the file?"

"Sure. I'll get Sandra to run one off." Wahlbergh went out again, and Alex lifted out what was left of a worn and faded blue canvas knapsack. It was dirty and shredded to ribbons, as if an animal had torn it to pieces, and there wasn't enough of it left to hold anything. Still, it gave Alex a strange feeling, holding the ragged piece of fabric his father had worn when he walked into the wilderness.

"Here you go. I'll need you to sign these forms." Wahlbergh handed over several papers and Alex scribbled his name in the places the policeman indicated. He thanked Wahlbergh and left the building. He wanted to be alone while he read whatever was in the file.

There was a bench outside, and he sat down, exchanging his glasses for the prescription sunglasses in his shirt pocket. Ivy had told him that April in Valdez often brought rain or even snow, but so far they'd been lucky. The sunlight glinting off the harbor was blinding. Alex sat looking out at the harbor for a moment, and then he opened the folder.

The first item was a letter from Alex's mother, Linda, to the Valdez police. It was dated September 15, 1972, saying that she was worried because Roy Nolan had said he'd be in touch the end of August, and so far he hadn't contacted her as he'd promised. She'd included a copy of one of the letters she'd given Alex, written by Roy from Valdez in late April of that year. In it, he assured her he'd be in touch the minute he came out of the bush.

There was also a copy of Roy's hand-drawn map

showing the route he'd planned to follow, and a photograph. Alex hadn't seen this particular one before. It was a head-and-shoulders shot, the type used in passports, and it was a profound shock to see his own mouth and jawline reflected in Roy's face.

Linda had followed the letter up with phone calls, and the troopers began an investigation. They'd sent out an all points bulletin with Nolan's picture on it. Valdez was small and there were names of half a dozen people who'd seen Roy in town that April—a waitress from some café, a man from the hostel, a clerk from the general store who'd sold him supplies.

Alex skimmed down the names and came to an abrupt halt, as an electric shock passed through his body.

Tom Pierce's name jumped off the page. Alex read the typewritten words and then read them again, hardly able to believe his eyes.

The report said that Tom had picked Nolan up early one morning, hitchhiking along the Richardson Highway. Pierce was believed to be the last person to speak to Roy Nolan.

CHAPTER NINE

This boat is full of characters. They all have an opinion, and they don't hold back telling you if they figure you're a fool. They seem to think they're the only ones who know much of anything.

From letters written by Roy Nolan,
April, 1972

PIERCE WAS BELIEVED to be the last person to speak to Roy Nolan.

Alex read that single sentence over and over before he finally was able to move on, his heart thundering.

In the police report, Pierce said that Roy had told him he'd worked his way to Valdez as a deckhand on a freighter. He was heading for the Alaskan interior, intending to walk deep into the bush and live off the land for a couple of months. Roy had ridden with him for about seventy miles, and Tom described in detail where he'd dropped him off. There was another hand-drawn map, probably made by Tom, indicating the place.

The last he saw of Roy Nolan, Pierce reported, he was standing on the side of the Thompson Highway. As far as the investigating officer could tell, Nolan had never been seen or heard from again.

His knapsack was found by a hiker late that fall, and it was surmised that a bear had been at it. The report concluded that Roy Nolan was officially a missing person, believed to be deceased.

A detailed list of the search operations followed. The area Roy's map covered had been divided into a grid, and planes had flown over, searching for him. Among the searchers, Tom Pierce.

Alex closed the folder and got to his feet. The next logical step was to talk to Ivy's father, and he wasn't looking forward to it.

TOM HAD JUST LANDED and taxied in to the dock. He saw Ladrovik standing there, obviously waiting for him. Tom swore and took his time shutting down and climbing out. He couldn't pinpoint why the young man got under his skin so bad, but he did, had from the moment he'd met him.

He hadn't known then that Ivy would take a shine to him. It had been Alex this and Alex that for the past week, and of course she'd dumped the doc. Which Tom figured probably meant there was something going on between her and this yahoo.

If Ivy had feelings for Ladrovik, there wasn't

much Tom could do, but he didn't have to like it. Besides, it wouldn't last, they never did. Ladrovik would head back to California at summer's end, and Tom knew Ivy wasn't about to leave Valdez.

What worried him was that she was going to get her heart broken one of these times, getting tangled up with no-account drifters from Away.

Ladrovik was walking toward him now. If he was here to try to butter him up, get on his good side because of Ivy, he was sadly mistaken. Tom clenched his teeth and smoothed his mustache.

"Tom, could I talk to you for a few minutes?"

"Talk away." Tom kept walking toward the trailer, a lot faster than was comfortable. To his shock, Ladrovik reached out and grabbed a handful of his wool jacket, pulling him to a stop.

"What the hell—"

"I just got this from the police station." Ladrovik held out a file folder.

"You got business with the cops, that's your problem." Tom didn't even glance down. He yanked his arm away and started to walk again.

Ladrovik followed. His voice was low, and there was something about it that made Tom think maybe the yahoo was tougher than he looked.

"It's about my father, my birth father," he said. "Roy Nolan. You remember Roy Nolan, don't you, Tom?"

Tom stopped so abruptly, Alex banged into him.

"Nolan? You're Nolan's kid?" Tom studied Alex's face through squinted eyes, feature by feature. The resemblance was there, from what he remembered. And what he remembered had given him nightmares for years.

Ladrovik nodded. "According to my mother I am, and she should know." His expression telegraphed to Tom that he wasn't making a joke.

Tom tried to hide his shock. "You don't use his surname."

"How could I? I didn't even know about him until six weeks ago, when my adoptive father died. I was two years old when my mother remarried. Up till then, my name was Jack Nolan. Steve insisted on changing it, Mom said. He wanted me to grow up thinking I was his son. And I did."

"Up here to find him, are you?" Tom made a derogatory noise in his throat. "Lots of luck, is all I can say. We searched for weeks, never found hide nor hair. And that was well over thirty years ago. Only thing ever turned up was that knapsack he was carrying."

"I know." Alex jerked a thumb at his own backpack. "The police gave it to me along with this file." He held the file out again. "It says here you were the last person to see Roy Nolan alive."

"And?" Bad as they were, Tom's nightmares had never stretched this far. In the first few years after

Nolan disappeared, Tom had wondered if some relative might turn up asking questions. But as the years passed, that particular fear had dissipated. The guilt never had. It was a guilt of omission, unlike others Tom had racked up over the years.

"I'd just like to know what he was like, what you talked about." When Tom didn't answer, Alex said, "Look, I'm naturally curious about my father. I'm trying to get a feel for the sort of man he was. Anything you remember would be helpful to me. And you don't have to sugarcoat anything, I just want the truth."

"It was a long time ago, I don't remember a whole lot," Tom lied, walking again. The truth was, he could recount practically word for word what had passed between him and Nolan that rainy morning. He sifted through the memories, tying to figure out how much to tell Ladrovik. "I was heading for Anchorage real early that April morning," he began. "Saw him standing on the side of the highway with his thumb out. It was raining, but there was still snow on the ground in the higher regions."

He remembered how his leg had hurt that morning. The injury was still new, and the pain had skewered up into his groin like a corkscrew pushing its slow way through flesh. He'd swallowed pain-killers, but they hadn't taken effect.

The hitchhiker had looked cold and wet, huddled inside a cheap parka. Tom figured he'd be someone to talk to, take his mind off his bloody leg.

"He was carrying a knapsack, had a rifle sticking out the side, looked like a .22. There was a sleeping bag tied on the bottom. Don't know how much grub he had, but it didn't look like a lot."

Tom had offered him coffee from a big steel thermos, and Nolan had thanked him. He'd wrapped his hands around the cup and taken deep gulps of the sweet hot liquid.

"A .22 isn't a very powerful gun," Alex commented. "It's not big enough to kill a moose or a bear, is it?"

"Nope. He might have had a bigger gauge weapon inside his pack, rolled in his sleeping bag. I didn't ask." Tom had reached the door of the office. He went in, praying that Bert or Kisha would be there to deflect this conversation.

The office was empty. Alex was right on his heels, and Tom had the feeling there wasn't enough air or space in the room for both of them.

"Did he say where he was going, what he planned to do?"

Tom shrugged, picked up a neat stack of paperwork Kisha had left for him. He pretended to study it. "Told me he was planning to walk into the bush and live off the land for a few months." Tom snorted. "Damn fool people from Outside, get some lame-brained idea in their head that they'll find the part of themselves they're missing if they come up here and go walkabout in the wilderness."

Alex's voice was soft. "Is that what Roy told you he was doing? That he was trying to find himself?"

Tom shook his head. "We didn't exactly get into the philosophy of life."

That, at least, was the truth. They'd talked politics instead. As the miles passed that morning, he and Nolan had gotten into a heated argument about Vietnam and the war.

Nolan was a peacenik, a Canadian hippie, scathingly critical of the U.S. policy in Vietnam. He said some things that were hard to defend, and Tom's anger had started to escalate.

With his leg throbbing, reminding him exactly where and how and why he'd gotten the piece of shrapnel that had crippled him forever, Tom soon lost his temper. He was still fiercely patriotic in those days. How could he admit the conflict he'd fought in was wrong? It would mean the two years he'd just spent in Vietnam, the injury he'd sustained, the friends he'd watched die…it would mean all of it was pointless. Wasted. Useless.

Nolan was oblivious. He'd gone on and on, a regular soapbox politician, until Tom's anger reached the boiling point. He'd slammed on the brakes and ordered the other man out of his truck.

And now his son wanted to know things.

"What did you talk about?"

Tom had to tamp down the panic the questions

raised. Damn fool wasn't about to give up. Tom put the desk between them and slumped into the chair.

"We talked wildlife, how best to live off the land."

That's what they should have talked about. Tom had been brought up in Alaska. He knew the other man wasn't dressed adequately even for a hike into the wilderness, never mind a long stay. He should've warned Nolan about the dangers, the bears just coming out of hibernation, the snow pack that still lay on the ground in most of the region, the rivers that would flood as it melted. He should've done his best to talk Nolan out of going anywhere.

"And did he seem to know much about camping and hunting?" Alex was still standing, leaning over with both hands propped on the desk, his smoldering eyes boring holes in Tom. "About living off the land?"

"Not a hell of a lot. It was too early in the season to try it, anyways." He should have insisted Nolan come back to Valdez, wait another week or two, get properly equipped. Instead, Tom had dumped him in the middle of nowhere, and if that wasn't bad enough, he didn't stop later that day and tell the Alaska State Troopers about Nolan.

Let the damned loudmouthed fool learn the hard way, Tom had fumed. Easy to talk about right and wrong when you've led a sheltered life. See what he has to say after he's been in the bush for a week or so, the know-it-all hippie.

He'd driven off and not even looked back. He'd ignored the unspoken law of the Arctic.

All men are brothers, regardless. And Nature is the common enemy.

He'd thought of Nolan a couple times that summer, but that was the summer Tom had met Frances, and he wasn't thinking much at all. He'd never really loved a woman before her. He'd never dreamed that any woman as beautiful as she was would give him a second look. But she had, and it threw him off balance.

And then that fall the police had sent out word Nolan was missing.

Tom had told them pretty much what he'd just told Alex. He'd spent untold hours and his own gas money flying back and forth and up and down the grid, covering Nolan's map east to west, north to south, hoping against hope that somebody would spot him, or that he'd turn up in Anchorage or Fairbanks. Skagway, maybe.

Autumn turned to winter, and that's when Tom's guilt had really taken hold. That's when he realized the other man was likely dead. And it was partly his fault.

"Not much else I can tell you. We searched for him all that fall."

"I know, I saw the details in the report." Alex straightened, rolling his shoulders to get the tension out. "I want to thank you for that. I read that you played a major part in the search."

Shame and guilt made Tom mean. "It's what we do up here, sonny, regardless that it's a waste of time and money and energy. You crackpots from the lower forty-eight who come North to live out some Jack London wet dream oughta be locked up. Or shipped back to California where you belong."

Alex's expression changed. The smoldering anger was back, hotter this time.

Tom had to force himself to keep on looking straight up into the younger man's face. It had been a mistake to sit, it put him at a disadvantage, but getting up again meant levering slowly and awkwardly out of the chair because his leg had gone numb. He wouldn't show weakness, not now.

"I don't know what you've got against me, Pierce." The words were quiet, the tone firm and cold. "If I've done something to piss you off, it wasn't deliberate and I apologize. But I've sure as hell had enough of your insults. Either level with me about what's biting your ass or get over it."

Tom held the other man's gaze, his own deliberately belligerent, but respect niggled at him all the same. It took guts to challenge a man on his own ground, especially when he had a daughter you fancied.

And of course Ivy would choose that exact moment to barge through the door.

CHAPTER TEN

The nights are long up here, Linda. I wake up and for a minute I think you're beside me. I really miss holding you.

From letters written by Roy Nolan,
April, 1972

"HEY, GUYS, what's up?"

Animosity must have been as thick as farts in the air, because she instinctively moved around the desk to stand beside him, one hand on his shoulder. "Dad? Alex? What's going on?"

Tom knew he was being an asshole. He just didn't know how to admit it. And he sure didn't want to get into it in front of Ivy.

But Alex had no such reservations.

His tone was cool. "I just found out that your father was the last person to see mine alive. I was asking him some questions about it."

"Your father?" Ivy frowned and shook her head.

"I don't get it. Dad's never been to San Diego, not for years. What do you mean, he was the last person to see your father alive?"

"Remember I told you, Steve Ladrovik was not my biological father," Alex said. And then he went on to tell her the whole story as he knew it.

It was obvious Ladrovik hadn't told Ivy any of his real reasons for being in Valdez. Tom could see the surprise on her face.

"So you really came up here to—to what, find your father?"

"Not find him, of course not." Ladrovik's voice was impatient. "I simply want to know whatever there is to know about him, and I plan to follow the route he took when he went into the bush. But I've got no illusions about finding him, that's not the point."

"So what were you and Dad arguing about? And what's this about Dad being the last one to see him alive?"

"It says so right here." Alex held out the file. She laid it on the desk and went through it, item by item. It seemed to take a long time.

"I never heard anything about this." She looked at Tom, her eyebrows raised in question. "Captain? You never mentioned this."

"No reason to," he blustered. "It happened long before you were ever born."

She slowly nodded. "So what were you two arguing about, then?"

There was a charged silence. Ladrovik gave Tom a look that said, *ball in your court.*

"I said something I maybe shouldn't have, about people coming here and getting lost." It was as far as Tom was willing or able to go.

Ivy narrowed her eyes at him. "Oh, yeah? Would that be your patented speech about brainless yahoos from Outside wasting everyone's time and money, Captain?"

Reluctantly, Tom said, "Something like that."

"Lucky Alex didn't deck you," Ivy said with a smile that looked more than a bit forced. "And now, Alex, if you two have finished butting heads, we'd better get back to the lodge. Mavis needs shortening for pastry—we're having meat pie for supper and God help me if I don't get it there in time."

"Bert said he'd give me a ride back in the boat."

"Well, Dad will tell him he doesn't have to bother, then, won't you, Dad? C'mon, Alex."

Tom watched as Alex retrieved the file and then held the door open for Ivy. He didn't look back as he followed her over to the copter pad.

Tom swung around so he could see out the window. It didn't look to him as if the two of them were doing much talking. Ivy'd been put out over something Alex said, all right, but Tom had no idea what it might be.

He lifted up the phone to call Frances, talk the

whole mess over with her, and then set it down again. It was far too late to look for comfort there. He'd burned his bridges with his wife as surely as he had with Roy Nolan—a long time ago.

You can't change the past, his mother used to say. She was a dour Scotswoman long dead now, but the older he grew the more her sayings would come back to haunt him. *You made your bed, Tommy. Now lie in it.*

And it was about as comfortable as a bed of nails.

IVY DIDN'T IMMEDIATELY begin the procedures leading to takeoff. Instead, she slowly fastened her safety belt, thinking over what she'd just learned about Alex.

It was hard to figure out why she felt betrayed and angry with him, but she did. She tried to remind herself that there was absolutely nothing between them, so she had no reason to get pissed at him for holding back on his reasons for being in Valdez. It didn't help.

"I don't get it," she finally burst out. "Why the secrecy, why not come out right up front and say why you were up here, Alex?"

As usual, his response was slow in coming. "I wasn't deliberately being secretive. I just didn't want to dump all my personal problems on everyone the moment I met them."

The trouble was, she didn't want to be lumped in with everyone. She wanted to be special. She wanted to be the one he'd choose to confide in. It bothered her that she felt that way and he obviously didn't.

Wouldn't you know that the one guy in a long while who really turned her on would be someone who wanted to disappear into the damned bush on some wild goose chase?

She started the rotors and went through the preflight routine. They were airborne before she looked at him again.

His face was chalky, and he was sweating and swallowing repeatedly. His eyes were closed and, with the force of a blow, it dawned on her that Alex was terrified. *He was afraid of flying.* She should have recognized the signs earlier that day, but she'd been preoccupied with pointing out the landscape. She'd just expected him to love the experience as much as she did.

He didn't have his earphones on, so she couldn't reassure him. She reached over and touched his knee to get his attention and get him to put on the headset.

But he only pointed at the control panel. Smoke was curling out in slow wispy streams.

Ivy's eyes flew to her controls. The oil pressure was fine, but the engine temp was running high. A red light began flickering, and the smoke from the panel grew thick.

She needed to get them on the ground. Tipping the copter sharply to the left, she scanned the landscape for a place to safely put down, hopefully a spot where Tom could also land with the floatplane.

She flicked the radio to the company frequency to alert him, but the radio wasn't responding. Heavy static gave way to a bleeping sound and then nothing. After several tries she gave up, concentrating instead on finding a spot to put down—fast.

She knew there was a small lake not far away. She turned the copter in that direction and, when she spotted a meadow not far from the water, Ivy put all her energy and attention into the landing.

How would the skids fit on the patch of meadow she'd chosen? With only one passenger and minimal cargo, she didn't have to worry about weight, but bringing the chopper down on new and unexplored territory was always a challenge. What if the ground was marshy, and the copter sank?

She had no choice. Adrenaline rushed through her as the earth came up to meet them. The copter bumped, lunged to the right a little, and then settled comfortably on the skids.

Ivy shut down the controls, and as the rotors slowed and the noise faded, she turned to Alex. Reaching across him, she unhooked his seat belt and then her own.

"Out, fast," she ordered. Smoke was still wafting

from the control panel and, as soon as he'd half tumbled out the door, she bailed out, too.

The ground was marshy, but fortunately there was still enough frost in the earth to make it firm. The copter would be okay here—if it didn't burst into flames. She watched for several minutes, half expecting it to happen, but the smoke gradually dissipated. She heaved a sigh of relief.

When she was pretty certain the machine wasn't going to explode or burn itself up, she looked for Alex.

He was a short distance away, bending over with his hands on his knees, his head hanging down.

"Sorry about that," she said. "There wasn't time to explain what I was doing. I don't think it was that serious, there's no sign of fire and the smoke is pretty much gone, but I had to put our safety first."

When he didn't raise his head or respond, she added, "I know it's a little late to tell you this, but we weren't ever in any real danger, no matter how it felt to you. As a safety precaution, I just had to get us down as fast as possible." She touched his arm. "Are you okay, Alex? Are you going to be sick?"

"I don't think so." He raised his head and gave her a facsimile of a grin. His face was still ashen. "Close, though."

"You really don't like flying, do you?"

"I hate it." He stood straight, flexing his shoulders, looking up and squinting into the blue afternoon sky.

"I have what amounts to a phobia about it. I get airsick even in huge commercial airliners. Why do you think I drove all the way from California?"

She nodded slowly. "So taking you up in the copter today—that wasn't exactly something you enjoyed, right?"

He looked at her and then he started to laugh, big belly guffaws that made her smile, even though she didn't understand what was funny.

When he got his breath, he said, "You have no idea how bad that was, Ivy. I'd never have willingly climbed into that beast if I wasn't trying so hard to impress you. If you weren't driving that thing, it would have taken a small army to hogtie me and chain me in the seat."

When that sank in, it was Ivy who felt like laughing, freed from the heavy weight inside her. "You let me take you up because you wanted to impress me? Why would you want to do that?"

He took two long steps toward her and pulled her into his arms. He was stronger than she'd guessed.

Ivy tensed in anticipation. Her pulse picked up as she slid her arms around him, aware of lean, hard muscle beneath his jacket. They were almost exactly the same height.

"Because from the first moment I met you, I've wanted to do this." He tipped her chin up with his knuckles and kissed her.

His mouth was hot and urgent on hers. She was trembling a little, and so was he. She could feel his hands, fingers spread apart, one at her waist, pulling her against him, one cupping the back of her head as if he thought there was a chance she might pull away.

As if.

Her lips softened and opened as the kiss deepened. He smelled like dental antiseptic and tasted of spearmint gum, and both were more arousing to her than any expensive male cologne.

"I thought you weren't interested," she whispered when the kiss ended.

"I was trying hard not to be." He drew her mouth back to his, and she gave herself over to sensation, the warmth of his lips, the taste of his tongue, the pulsing desire that made her want to get closer and still closer.

"Why would you try not to be?"

"It's complicated." He released her and stepped back. "So what do we do now, Ivy? Will someone come along and rescue us?"

She felt let down all over again. This guy was a regular roller-coaster ride.

"Eventually, yes, someone will come. It won't be for a while, because the radio failed just before we landed. And cell phones don't work up here in the mountains. But Dad will realize something's wrong and come and find us. Now, about this complication you mentioned?"

"You don't give up, do you, Pierce?" He said it gently, with a smile.

"Never."

He looked straight into her eyes. "I was divorced a couple of years ago, I think I told you that."

"Yeah, you did. So, what's up with that? There's a new lady in San Diego? You're still in love with your ex?" She could get him over either of those, given half a chance. Maybe.

"No. There's no one back there. As for Rebecca, we're friends, but I'm not in love with her."

"Then what?"

"We had a little girl. Annie. Anne Marie." When he said the name, his voice deepened, became tender. "She'd just turned three when she got an ear infection. The doctor gave her medication, but she died a day later. Some rare form of meningitis."

"Oh, Alex. I'm so sorry." She hadn't imagined anything like that.

His smile was both rueful and sad. "Yeah. Me, too."

She thought maybe she shouldn't ask, but she did anyway. "Is that why your marriage ended?"

He nodded slowly. "Yeah, pretty much. Looking back, I can see that we probably weren't ever that solid, and losing Annie was more than we could handle. Instead of turning to one another, we went in different directions." He looked out at the lake. "Whatever the reason, it's not something I'd get into again, Ivy. Not ever."

She swallowed hard. "Marriage, you mean? Or kids?"

"Either. Both."

"My mom and dad lost a child a long time ago. My brother, Jacob. He was five when he died. I was two and a half, so I don't have any real memories of him."

She could see that caught his attention. "Do they still talk about him?"

"Dad does. Mom never mentions Jacob, at least not to me. She doesn't talk about the past much at all."

"Some people can't bear the reminder. But for me, it helps to talk about Annie. She's part of me, she always will be."

The tenderness in his tone brought tears to her eyes. She waited, wanting him to describe his daughter for her.

But instead he said, "I haven't met your mother. I know she and your dad are still together because I've heard the Galloways refer to her, but you never talk about her."

"Don't I?" It wasn't really a surprise. "Well, I don't see her all that often, we're very different. And we've never gotten along all that well. We sort of go our separate ways. It's pretty much my dad who holds our family together."

"Doesn't she like to fly?"

"Who, my mother?" She wondered why he would ask that…if he was somehow sympathizing with Frances. "She's okay with it." Ivy shrugged. "She can take it or leave it. She's not passionate like Dad and I are. See, Frances was a supermodel before her and Dad got married. She's more interested in clothes and makeup than she is in anything else. She teaches a night-school course, a makeover thing. It's pretty popular with the girls and women in Valdez."

"But not with you?"

She wrinkled her nose. "I never cared much about how I looked. All that makeup stuff and fancy clothes just reminds me of gift-wrapping." And besides, there really wasn't any point. Ivy knew from early childhood she'd never measure up to her mother, so she'd never tried.

"You don't have to care." He stroked her hair, letting his hand linger in the short curls.

His touch sent shivers down her spine. Damn, he really turned her on. But he was devious, he kept secrets. She hated secrets.

"You sure don't need gift-wrapping," he breathed. His eyes searched her face feature by feature.

She felt heat spread across her cheeks. Her mother called blushing the redhead's curse.

"Thank you." Talking about her looks always

made Ivy nervous. Maybe he guessed, because he changed the subject.

"A supermodel, wow. How did she end up in Alaska?"

She figured he also meant why had Frances married Tom. It was a question Ivy's teenage friends hadn't been as reticent about asking. After all, the life of a New York supermodel and that of an Alaskan-born Vietnam vet didn't hold many similarities.

"Like I said, my mother isn't exactly Chatty Cathy. From the little she's told me, she came up with a crew sent by a fashion magazine, I think it was *Vogue,* to do a photo shoot. They hired my dad to fly them around, show them the countryside, find interesting backdrops for the photos. I guess he and my mom fell madly in love. Frances stayed when the crew went back to New York, and they got married." She'd never really understood it herself, because she couldn't remember Tom and Frances ever acting as if they were madly in love. She'd always wondered about that. Maybe it was just sex, because when you figured out Jacob's birthdate and their wedding anniversary, it was obvious Frances had been pregnant.

Alex was looking around for a place to sit. "I had problems with my stepfather, so I understand a bit about you and your mom. You're pretty close to your father, though."

She relaxed and smiled. Here she was confident.

"Yes, we're really close. We always have been. He's been my best buddy since I was a little kid."

He bent over and touched the ground, rubbing his hand on his pant leg when it came up wet. "So any guy in your life would have to make the grade with Tom."

"No." That irritated the hell out of her, and she scowled at him. "Absolutely not. Any guy in my life would have to make the grade with *me.* My father doesn't choose who I date."

"Maybe he doesn't choose." He looked her straight in the eye. "But he'd have to live up to the standard Tom has set. That's a pretty tall order."

She couldn't deny that. She *did* use her father as a measuring stick of sorts. What was wrong with that? "Why are you concerned or even interested, Professor? You've made it clear any involvement with me is off your radar."

He took his time answering. "I didn't say that. I said that marriage and babies aren't part of my plans."

"So what are you proposing then, Ladrovik? Hot, steamy sex for a couple of weeks and then a civilized goodbye?" God, the arrogance of him. "Because just like you have this thing about long-term commitment, I have my own rules about casual affairs. I don't do short-term." Not usually. Well, not anymore. It left her far too empty and lonely afterwards.

"Guess that rules out anything between us, then." His voice was wistful. He reached out and rubbed his thumb across her lips. "But damn it all, I want you, Ivy," he whispered, his eyes trapping hers, holding them against her will. "I can't help it. I want to taste you, touch you everywhere."

She couldn't stop a powerful shiver of awareness, the rush of warmth and desperate need.

He groaned and pulled her back into his arms. This time the kiss bordered on brutal, but it was an embrace between equals. Ivy knew she was every bit as rough as he was, as demanding and consumed by desire. She gave him back kiss for kiss, pressing the length of her body against him, holding him as tight as he held her.

Maybe it was the aftermath of danger, but she wanted him to take her there and then, rip off her jeans and tumble with her to the damp grass. Her desire was mindless and all-consuming, and she was frantic with it. When his hands dipped under her leather jacket and cupped her breasts, she trapped them, pressing them against her aching nipples.

"Yes," she murmured, leaning hard against him and trembling so that she could barely stand. She could feel his erection, and she dropped her hand to his zipper, desperate to release him. It was hard to get the zipper down, but she managed. And gasped as loud as he did when her hand held the length of him. Which is why she didn't hear the floatplane until it was almost directly overhead.

CHAPTER ELEVEN

It's funny, what you miss when your old lady's not around. Sex, for sure. But just talking, I miss that. Nobody ever listened to me the way you do, Lindy.

From letters written by Roy Nolan,
April, 1972

"WIRE ON THE PANEL SHORTED out," Tom announced three quarters of an hour later. "Can't see anything else wrong." He and Bert had gone over the copter inch by inch.

Ivy had stayed near them, while Alex wandered down to the lake where the floatplane was gently bobbing. She wondered if he felt as off balance as she did. The arrival of her father and Bert had prevented them from having crazy monkey sex right on the ground, but she couldn't just turn off the wild emotions.

"Ivy?"

She realized that her father had called her more than once. He repeated with more than a trace of impatience, "Listen up. I said, you two can take the Beaver back to the lodge. Bert and I will fly the copter to Anchorage—it's overdue for servicing anyways. Ben's in visiting Theo, so we'll hitch a ride back into town with him."

"Sure, that's fine with me." The sooner she got away from Tom, the better. He'd given her a narrow-eyed look when he and Bert landed, and she was aware that Tom had studiously avoided either looking at or speaking to Alex. She knew her father and Bert had seen them from the air, groping one another.

She could understand Tom being mildly embarrassed at the sight of his daughter making out, but that didn't account for the way he was acting. He was being downright rude to Alex, and it annoyed her. It also puzzled her. Tom could be—was often—acerbic, but he wasn't a rude man by nature.

"This is your lucky day, Professor," she called to Alex as she saw him approach—trying hard for a light note. "Now you get to ride in the floatplane." She explained what was happening. "We have to transfer the supplies. Mavis is going to be hopping mad at us for not getting the shortening there on time for supper."

There was only one load each, but they had to wade in the icy water to stow it in the floatplane.

By the time Ivy was settled in the cockpit, her pants were wet past her knees and her boots were sopping. Alex was as wet as she was. He was sitting next to her in the copilot's seat, and this time he was making no effort to pretend this flight was going to be something he enjoyed. He was already holding on to the roof strap, and he turned and gave her a comically doleful look.

"I don't suppose I could walk back, huh?"

She shook her head and smiled at him before she started the motor. It was tough for her to sympathize, because flying was as comfortable to her as breathing.

"This won't take long," she assured him. "Just think of it as a root canal."

He shot her a look. "If there was any other way to get back, I'd take it."

She laughed outright. "If you're going to be sick, there's a bucket in the back," she consoled him, and then she concentrated on getting them airborne.

The days were getting longer, Alex mused later that evening. Even though there were clouds gathering out over the water, at past ten at night it was still twilight. From his perch on the dock, he could still clearly see the outline of trees across the bay and the sleek shape of an eagle sitting on a stump. Birds twittered, and he could hear several guests at the lodge talking and laughing, having a smoke and a nightcap out on the wide deck. But down here by the water he was alone, and glad of it.

Well, almost alone. He couldn't discount the mosquitoes. He swatted at one buzzing around his ear. He'd quit smoking years ago when Rebecca first became pregnant with Annie, but at this moment he longed for the comfort of a cigarette—and the nicotine smoke that would drive away these pesky insects.

He'd learned some surprising things today about his father. And about Ivy's father as well.

He grimaced at the thought of Tom. The older man had made it crystal-clear he despised him, although Alex had no idea what the reason was, apart from his relationship with Ivy. Or lack thereof, he amended with an ironic sigh.

He'd been ready to take her standing up, out there in the meadow. He'd been half out of his mind with…he searched for the word. Lust? Desire? Sexual frustration? All of them. And she'd been just as wild as he. Just thinking about her hand on him made him hard all over again.

And then he'd disgraced himself in front of her. His eyes flicked to the Beaver, floating at the end of the dock, securely moored and tied down. If he had his way, he'd never set foot in any type of aircraft again, particularly not a floatplane or, God help him, a helicopter.

He heard boots on wood and turned to look.

Ivy was striding along the dock, holding two cans of beer.

"Want a nightcap?" She held out a can. He took it

and she sat on the dock beside him, dangling her legs over the side. Her shoulder brushed against him and he caught a whiff of some fruity-smelling shampoo.

He was glad he was sitting.

"Thanks." He popped the tab and took a long drink.

"I saw you sneak away after KP, when I got corralled into talking about global warming with that environmental guy from Canada."

"I noticed that. I think he wants to do more than talk about global warming with you." Alex had felt something very much like jealous rage when Simon took Ivy's arm and herded her away from the others.

"*No.* You think?" She widened her eyes and grinned at him. He could barely stop himself from grabbing her shoulders and kissing that teasing smirk away.

"About today, Ivy." He wasn't sure what he wanted to say, but he knew they needed to talk. And like the coward he'd proven himself to be, he avoided the real issue. "Sorry for being such a wimp about flying."

"Don't apologize. We all have things we're afraid of."

"You don't seem to be afraid of anything."

"Oh, yeah? Shows how much you know. My list is lengthy." She took a long pull on her beer. "To begin with, I hate crowds and noise. I get so nauseous and dizzy and scared I feel like I'm going to pass out."

"So you don't like cities."

"Nope." She sipped her beer and shook her head.

"Frances once took me to New York—it was supposed to be a big treat for my sixteenth birthday. I've never been that miserable in my life. And cranky. Boy, was I cranky. I know most people love to travel—look at the hordes of tourists who flock up here. But not me. That's why I've stayed here ever since that trip, where there's wide open spaces and quiet places."

He wondered if he'd understood correctly. "You've only been south once?"

She gave him a puzzled look. "Of course. Once was enough to find out I didn't like it. Why would I do it again?"

"To give yourself a second chance? If you've only ever been to New York—"

"I've been to Anchorage, I don't like it there, either. Did going up in the floatplane change your mind about flying in the helicopter?"

She had him there. "Can't say it did."

"So maybe diversity isn't a sure cure, huh?"

"Maybe not." Why was it so important to him to convince her that *south* wasn't a dirty word? "It's just that there are other places besides New York. San Diego has the Pacific Ocean, miles of parks, lots of quiet places." He hesitated. "But if you're happy here, I guess there's no real reason to travel."

"My attitude exactly." She swatted a mosquito and tipped the can to her lips. He watched, mesmerized by the shape of her mouth, the movement of her throat, the swell of her breasts beneath the long-sleeved flannel shirt.

"About today, Ivy. Before help arrived."

"Are you going to apologize again?"

He couldn't read her expression. "I wasn't planning on it. You?"

"Me, apologize?" She shook her head and gave a muffled chuckle that turned into a snort. "I don't think so."

He cleared his throat. His voice was gruff. "Then I was thinking more along the lines of taking up where we left off."

He saw her cheeks stain with rich color, and he heard her catch her breath. "I'd have to think about that. I told you my policy on short-term passion."

"You did. But policies change. If yours should happen to be open for revision, you know where to find me." He got to his feet and walked down the dock and up the steps without so much as a glance back at her.

MUCH LATER, Ivy heard the rain start. It pattered a gentle rhythm on the roof of her little cabin, and it should have been soothing. She pulled the comforter closer around her shoulders and listed all the reasons against getting involved with Alex. He was from Away, he hated flying, he wasn't long-term, he was planning some harebrained scheme that involved going walkabout in the bush…. And to say Tom disliked him was an understatement. Captain had looked ready to throw a punch in the office today.

And that gnawed at her. Alex had struck a nerve when he'd told her she'd need her father's stamp of approval. Was she really that influenced by Tom and his opinions? Alex wouldn't be around long enough to even cause ripples. Would she be sorry for what she hadn't done, after he was gone?

Ten minutes of pondering had her rummaging in a drawer for supplies she hadn't needed for some time. Did condoms have a best-before date? She hoped not as she shoved several in her pocket. She pulled on a jacket and hoped Alex wasn't in the habit of locking his cabin door.

CHAPTER TWELVE

I hope you're not mad anymore. This is something I've got to do before I settle down with you and the sprout.

From letters written by Roy Nolan,
April, 1972

ALEX WAS DREAMING. He was able to fly, no plane, no nothing. No fear, even. Just his body and the ability to move it at will through the air. He was soaring over the Arctic landscape, arms spread wide, dipping up and down.

He was searching for Roy Nolan who'd somehow morphed into Tom Pierce.

The feeling of euphoria evaporated when the click of the latch on the cabin door brought him instantly awake. He sat up, squinting to see. There was a faint glow through the windows of the cabin, but not enough to really make out who it was that quietly closed the door. He groped for his glasses and then paused when he heard, "Alex? Don't shoot, it's me."

Ivy slid her jacket off and dropped it on a chair. “It’s raining, hear it on the roof?”

She ran her hands through her hair and then dried them on her pants. She stumbled over his boots and cursed under her breath. Giggling, she bent to tug her own off, hopping to keep her balance. She dropped them to the wooden floor with a clunk.

Half believing he was still dreaming, praying fervently that he wasn’t, he stood and reached for her, hands closing on the soft skin of her upper arms.

“Ivy. God, Ivy, I’m so glad you’re here.”

She came readily into his embrace. She smiled at him, reached her hands up and cupped his face with her fingers, then pressed her mouth against his. Her hands slid up and skimmed through his hair, traced the shape of his ears and neck.

The fire that had been smoldering inside him ever since that afternoon when he’d first kissed her ignited now. As her tongue chased his, she moaned and fumbled for the bottom of his T-shirt and tried to haul it over his head, but Alex resisted.

“Not so fast.” All the decisions so far had been hers. Now it was his turn, and he was determined to make this good. He might not be a hero when it came to flying, but *this* he knew how to do—and it was what he wanted, more than anything in the world at this moment. And he wanted it perfect.

But she was in such a hurry, going slow was a challenge. His body urged him to tumble with her to the bunk, pull down her loose pants and slide—he swallowed hard. This was a time for distraction, just enough so he wouldn't disgrace himself yet again.

So he concentrated only on her lips, kissing her, at first shallow, then deeper, exploring her mouth in every way he could devise. He nibbled kisses along her throat, took her earlobe in his mouth and sucked, kissed her eyes, her nose, back to her mouth, deeper this time, longer. She was making little sounds in her throat, urgent moans that signaled desire. Sounds that once again threatened to send him over the edge.

"Easy, pretty lady." He slid a hand up under the loose T-shirt she wore, finding her bare breasts, teasing a nipple with his thumb and forefinger. He pulled the shirt off before bending his head and suckling, drawing her nipple deeply into his mouth, using his tongue on the hard tip.

"Alex, let's lie down." Her voice was hoarse and urgent.

"Yeah, let's." He maneuvered them toward the bunk, tossing the blankets back.

Rain pattered and then grew harder, hammering down on the roof as they undressed one another, slowly at first, and then with an abandon that matched the storm outside.

When his boxers were off and he could feel the smoothness of her belly and thighs against his flesh, Alex yanked off his shirt and then tugged her bikini underwear off. Then he simply held her against him, half drunk with sensation, hungry for more, reluctant to ever get to the end.

She whispered, “In my pants pocket, I have a—”

“So do I.” He touched her with his eyes closed, letting his hands and lips blindly discover her narrow waist, the swell of hips, the hot wetness between her thighs.

She was moaning louder, making inarticulate noises as he suckled and teased and licked.

“Now, Alex. Right now.” She wrapped her legs around his hips, reached down and guided him into her.

Ivy held on as if he were a life raft.

Somehow he knew her body. He knew where to touch, to kiss, he sensed the rhythm that would suit her. There was no awkwardness, no hesitation, just an escalating, encapsulating rapture as he slid into her and, with maddening slowness, dipped deeper and still deeper.

There was no room for anything but sensation. Nothing but glorious intensity, which grew and grew until it lifted her up to an unbelievable height. Her orgasm rocked her, wave after wave of sensation that made her cry out with joy—and drew him with her into release.

They collapsed together, boneless, mindless. Ivy was trembling.

"You cold, sweetheart?" He pulled the comforter up and tucked it around her shoulders, turning her in his arms so that she fit against his chest. "Easy, darling. Easy. Relax."

His gentleness brought tears to her eyes. In a moment she'd have to remind herself that this was very temporary, that she'd broken her own rules by inviting herself here, that it could only be a flight without a destination.

But for the moment there were only these delicious tremors, euphoria and Alex's body, wrapping her close and keeping her warm and safe.

They made love again, gentle, slow, as early-morning light filtered through the screened windows and the birds called to one another. In the dim light, Ivy noticed the photo of the little girl. The professional portrait in a plain wooden frame was propped against a stack of books on the small nightstand at the foot of the bunks.

Ivy picked it up and studied it. She knew Alex was watching.

"Annie." It wasn't a question. The child looked about three, a sober little girl in a fussy blue dress. She'd refused to smile for the camera, and Ivy admired her for that. She had her father's eyes, black, disconcerting in such a little person. And his jawline, strong and square. Hers had an enchanting dimple, though. Her hair must have come from her mother, black and impossibly thick, long and curly.

"Yeah, that's my Annie Marie." The tenderness in his tone broke her heart.

"She hated dresses, Rebecca insisted she put that one on for the photo and she was not happy about it."

"I can tell." It reminded Ivy of herself as a little girl, when Frances forced her to put on something that didn't match Ivy's image of herself.

"I have some snapshots that are more like her than that one." He put his glasses on and dug into a pack on the floor, handing over a small photo album, the kind studios handed out when they developed negatives.

"You're shivering, get in here and cover up," he ordered. "You can look at them while I light the heater."

He wrapped her in the blankets, and she held the album unopened as she watched him pull on sweats and a heavy shirt. His body was that of a runner, broad-shouldered but long and lithe, with muscles that weren't evident under clothes. There was an elegance about him, a certain balance of proportion that pleased her.

He knelt to crumple paper, and she opened the album.

It was a record of Annie's short life. In the first photo, she was just born, red and puffy and wonderfully ridiculous with an outraged expression and a full thatch of dark hair into which someone had stuck a pink bow.

"Ah, she's brand new here," Ivy breathed.

"She weighed almost ten pounds...she was a bruiser."

She turned the page. Here, the baby was an adorable three months or so, propped against a pile of pillows, smiling at the camera.

The next photo was obviously a record of her first step. Her dark eyes were wide and intense, and she had her arms spread out and a look of utter concentration on her face as she lunged toward the camera.

There were birthday photos of Annie with icing on her chin, in her hair, on both hands. In another she was being cuddled by a petite woman in a policeman's uniform. Mother and baby had identical black curls and pouty, rosebud smiles.

"That's Rebecca," Alex confirmed. Ivy figured he must have been glancing over at the snapshots in between feeding kindling into the stove.

"She's a police officer?"

"Not anymore. Now she does grief counseling."

Ivy studied the other woman, how pretty she was. Lavishly rounded, she was a very feminine woman, which the tailored uniform emphasized.

Suddenly she was very conscious of her short hair, her tall, boyish body, her small breasts.

The last photo was a family shot. Alex was

wearing a white golf shirt and casual slacks, holding Annie in one arm with his other around Rebecca. Annie had her cheek pressed against her father's, and all three of them were smiling.

"That was just weeks before she died." Alex was crouched beside the bunk.

"You all look so happy."

"We were, in that moment." His voice was wistful. "Maybe that's all we ever get in life, just fleeting moments when we actually recognize we're happy."

"Maybe you're right." She handed the album back to him and looked at the clock. It was just past five. "Yikes, I've got to get moving or the whole place will know I spent the night with you."

"I don't mind if you don't."

"I've carved out a reputation as a vestal virgin, no point in destroying the illusion." She wrapped the sheet around her. "Besides, Mavis isn't going to be happy with me unless I get over to the kitchen and help with breakfast. And then I'm taking Oliver and two fishermen to a river high in the mountains."

"Even in the rain?" It was still coming down, lighter than it had in the night, but steady.

"Fishermen actually think fish bite better in the rain, go figure." She made a move toward the bathroom.

"Wait." He caught her and held her against him, sheet and all. "Ivy, last night was—" He searched for a word but came up empty. He kissed her instead.

Ivy closed her eyes and let herself get lost in sensation again, just for a moment. "I wish we could spend the day right here," he whispered.

She pressed her nose to his neck, sniffing in the scent that was his individual signature with a lot of her mixed in. "I wish so, too," she confessed.

"Will you visit me again tonight?"

"I'm not sure." How many times could you use a potent drug without becoming addicted? "Being with you could easily become a habit, Professor. That wouldn't be the best thing for either of us, now would it?"

She waited for him to deny it.

He didn't. Instead he slowly released her. "I'll make us some coffee while you're in the shower."

"That would be great." She kept her tone cheerful and light, but she wished she could just pull her clothing on and head straight out to the floatplane. She felt unsettled, and there was an ache in her stomach. She wanted to climb in the Beaver, focus on procedure.

Flying was the only thing that always made her feel better.

One thing about having short hair, showering was fast. The coffee was ready by the time she was done, just as he'd promised. She took the mug he offered and said, "So what's on your agenda for today?"

"I want to get the cabins framed now the foundations are poured. I'd like to have them finished before Theo gets back, so he doesn't get any ideas about working on them himself. Have you heard when he's coming home?"

"Nobody knows for sure. I talked to Sage last evening, the doctors have him on a new medication. Caitlin told Sage it'll probably be another ten days at least. Aunt Cait's anxious to come home, and I know he is, too."

"It must be tough on them to be away from the lodge. This place is their life."

"It sure is." Ivy paused and then said, "How about you, are you feeling homesick, Alex?"

He looked surprised. In typical fashion he thought the question over before he replied. "Not at all. I like it here."

"Enough to stay?" Now why had she asked that? The last thing she wanted was to appear needy. "Not that it's a good idea, staying up here. Lots of people come for a visit in the summertime, fall in love with Alaska and decide to move here, but most of them don't make it through the first winter. Too dark, too depressing, too cold."

Which is what divided the natives from the visitors. True Alaskans loved the northern winter as much as they did the summer.

"Well, I'm not making any plans along those lines," he said. "I'm not making any plans at all, come to that. I'm pretty much taking my life one day at a time." He smiled at her. He had the best smile. It took away the serious demeanor his glasses gave him. "Live in the now, isn't that the popular expression?"

"It's a good idea, if you can do it." She gulped the remainder of her coffee, pulled her boots on and stood. "I have to find some clean clothes and then I'll see you at the lodge for breakfast." She was out the door before he could reply.

At the window, Alex watched her sprint through the trees to her cabin. When she disappeared, he turned slowly, aware that as always, Ivy left a hollow space behind her. The room felt empty without her in it.

He poured himself another coffee and sat at the table, trying to figure out what he was feeling. *Hungry, and not for food.* Guilty? Reluctantly, he admitted it to himself.

He should have thought through the implications before they made love, not after. She was a wildly passionate woman, but it wasn't only passion between them. In spite of their differences, there was a bond between them that wasn't just sexual. He wanted to know her better. He wanted to confide in her, tell her things that didn't much matter to anyone except him. He wanted, of all things, to meet Ivy's mother, to learn for himself how her influence had shaped Ivy into the woman she was.

He felt a connection with Ivy he didn't want to

feel. Not here, not now. He was here on a journey of self-discovery. Feelings for Ivy would simply distract him. He finished the coffee and rinsed the cup in the sink, but he couldn't clear his mind of Ivy as easily.

Or her father. Tom Pierce was a formidable force in his daughter's life, and Alex knew that the older man would be relieved if he, like Roy Nolan, disappeared and was never heard from again.

Something had been niggling at him ever since his heated conversation with Tom the previous day. The whole time they'd talked, Alex sensed that Tom was hiding something, holding something back. What had really happened that early spring morning along the deserted highway? Could Tom have had something to do with Roy's death?

Alex dismissed that as ridiculous. Pierce might be a prickly son of a bitch, but he wasn't a murderer. He'd have had nothing to gain from murdering Roy, for one thing. It wasn't as if Nolan had a wad of money, or anything else of value. His letters proved that he'd made the trip on a shoestring, leaving most of his money behind in an account for Linda.

And for him. Alex recognized that Nolan had tried, in some misguided fashion, to provide for them. It touched him, that Nolan had made that gesture.

But what had drawn the man so powerfully to this wild and beautiful country? What was he searching for as he walked into the wilderness? Self-discovery? Escape? Enlightenment?

Maybe all three. And what was prompting Alex to follow in his footsteps? Self-discovery. Escape. Enlightenment, whatever that might be.

Or death? It wasn't the first time Alex had entertained that thought.

As a child and a young teen, he'd been stubborn, willful, reckless, and he'd been beaten severely for it. Steve, an autocratic man and a disciplinarian, used first a belt and then his fists, arousing in Alex a confusing combination of fury, a hunger to please and overwhelming resentment toward his brother and sister who were never treated the way he was.

Dmitri and Zelda had none of the conflicts with their father that Alex had, and he not so jokingly referred to himself as the bad seed. In his midteens, he'd turned to running as a way to release frustration, and he'd started winning races, the only thing about Alex that had ever pleased Steve. Alex and his stepfather had forged an uneasy truce at race meets. Steve supported him by buying him the best shoes, but his approval was conditional on winning. When Alex lost, Steve verbally berated him and finally Alex had had enough. After he graduated and went on to university, he severed ties with his family.

He resented his mother for not defending him in the conflicts with Steve. And he'd never been especially close to his brother and sister. Linda did her best to keep in touch, but Alex formed new relationships at school, finding an acceptance he'd never had at home.

But after he and Rebecca were married, she made a point of including his family in their lives whenever possible. Annie needed an extended family, she'd insisted.

Linda had doted on Annie, her first and still her only grandchild. Later, she, and Steve as well, had clumsily tried to console Alex when Annie died. He shut them out. He shut everyone out. His world had crumbled around him, and for some time he didn't want to live. Oddly enough, it was Steve who suggested he start running again. He did, and gradually it helped.

Steve's death six weeks before had been unexpected, and his mother's revelation after the funeral had stunned Alex. It had also answered questions he'd had all his life about why he didn't fit into his family, why he felt alien, why he and his father not only had nothing in common, but didn't even like one another.

He was here in Alaska because for the first time in his life, he had an identity he could relate to, however nebulous. He had a hunger that bordered on neurosis to learn about this stranger who had willed him his genetic makeup. At first, he'd tried and failed to find any relatives in Canada who might give him a sense of the man. So he'd come here, to walk the labyrinth, follow in his father's footsteps.

And he couldn't let himself be distracted. Not by Ivy, not by anyone. He needed to put an end to the inner anguish that had held him captive since Annie's death. And, if he was honest, even before that.

Unless he did, and until he did, he wasn't whole.

CHAPTER THIRTEEN

I wish I could remember that poem you read to me once, about men being unwise and going to Samarkand.

From letters written by Roy Nolan,
April, 1972

ALL THAT DAY, doing her tourist patter, landing and taking off again, Ivy told herself she didn't need Alex. Admiring the fishermen's catch, loading the smelly men and their smelly fish into the floatplane, she repeated it like a mantra.

I don't need Alex. So he's good in bed, smart and funny, easy on the eyes. I like him fine, but I don't need him.

Late that afternoon, she skimmed across the water in the Beaver and came to a stop right where she'd planned, a few feet from the dock in front of the lodge. She turned off the motor, secured the plane and then helped the fishermen off. As they wandered up, she and Oliver unloaded rain gear, fishing rods, empty lunch containers and foam coolers loaded with fish and ice into transportable plastic bins to take up. And the whole time she worked, Ivy realized she was listening for the sound of a hammer and glancing toward the newly framed cabins.

He wasn't there, and he wasn't at supper, either.

"Where's Alex disappeared to?" Ivy hoped she sounded casual as she brought a tray of empty salad bowls back from the dining room and started ladling beef stew, mashed potatoes and gravy onto dinner plates. "I was kind of counting on him to help with dishes."

"He's gone with Bert to town." Mavis spooned peas and carrots on each plate as Ivy handed them to her. "Bert came with the boat and they took off a couple hours ago."

"Did Alex say when he'd be back?"

"Later tonight, was all he said." Mavis finished the last plate and joined Ivy in loading them on serving trays. "I can see you're sweet on him, honey. Saw you running like a rabbit from his cabin early this morning."

Ivy felt herself turning magenta. She concentrated hard on the trays.

"Just take care of yourself. These guys from Away are here today, gone tomorrow." Mavis pursed her mouth. "Mind you, all men are slippery buggers when it comes down to it."

Ivy was still trying to figure out what part of that to address when Mavis added, “I never met a man who didn’t have a fatal flaw, and that’s the truth.” She smacked a plate on the tray with more force than was necessary. “And Lord knows I’ve fallen for their blarney often enough myself.”

Ivy was flabbergasted. She’d never heard Mavis talk about men. She knew from Aunt Cait that Mavis had been married to a man from Seattle, and that the louse dumped her when she got burned, but that was all she’d ever heard of Mavis’s background, except that she and Caitlin had been friends from childhood.

“You sure he’s not married?” Mavis flopped the last plate down and studied Ivy. “Some of ’em will lie, you know.”

“He’s divorced.” Ivy was feeling defensive. “And that fatal flaw thing, Mavis? I know what you mean, but there are guys who don’t have it. Take Uncle Theo and Dad, for instance. They seem pretty stable to me.”

Mavis gave a telling grunt and turned away.

“What, you don’t think so?”

After a long moment, Mavis said, “You’re right, honey. Your uncle and your dad are exceptions. Now why don’t you get these out there while they’re still hot and people are still hungry.”

Later that night, Ivy thought over that conversation as she made her way to her cabin through the rain. The fatal flaw theory just wasn’t something she'd expected from Mavis. It hinted at depths she'd never suspected the other woman possessed. When Cait came home, she was going to ask her about Mavis. Working closely with her had been exasperating, but she'd always been fond of the eccentric little woman. Exactly how had she ended up a recluse here at Raven Lodge? Mavis went to town maybe twice a year. The rest of the time she stayed right here.

Through the sheets of rain teeming down, Ivy saw the copter sitting on its pad and felt a rush of affection. Planes represented freedom to her. She just wasn't a person rooted to the ground.

She wasn't a water person, either, and although she was competent at flying the Beaver, her heart belonged to the Bell. Tom had flown the copter back after supper, bringing Ben and Sage from Anchorage. Then he'd taken the float back to Valdez.

For Ivy it was also a huge relief to have her cousins back. They'd taken over the socializing part of the evening with the guests, making it possible for her to slip away early.

She looked over at Alex's cabin, but it was dark and obviously deserted. Well, even if he'd been there, she wasn't about to knock on his door again tonight. He'd pretty much made it plain that a one-night stand was all he was interested in. She had her pride, after all.

Damn men anyway. Mavis was probably right. Fatally flawed, every last one of them. She slammed the door on her cabin. Turning on the small lamp by the bed, she put a stack of cowboy ballads on her portable CD player and then knelt to shove paper and kindling into the heater. It wasn't that cold, but it was clammy.

She opened the damper on the stove and lit it, hanging up her jacket and tugging off her track shoes as the kindling crackled and popped. She felt restless. Maybe a hot shower would calm her down.

She shucked off her clothes, turned up the music and stood under the hot water. Each cabin had only a small hot water tank, so she was darned well going to enjoy every last drop.

The tiny bathroom filled with steam and gradually the water ran cool. Ivy stepped out before it got frigid, toweled off and was wrapping herself in her bathrobe when Alex appeared in the bathroom doorway.

Startled, she let out a shriek.

"Sorry, sorry, I didn't mean to scare you. I knocked and hollered, but I guess you didn't hear me." He had to raise his voice above the music still playing on the boom box.

He was near enough that she could smell the beer on his breath, although he didn't appear to be drunk. There were raindrops on his glasses and in his hair. He reached out and touched her throat with the back of his fingers, and alarms went off in every nerve ending.

"What—what are you doing here, Alex?" Damn, now the man had her stammering. And asking stupid questions.

"I thought about you all day." His voice was low and intense. "I just couldn't get you out of my mind." He cupped the back of her neck and drew her closer. "But I'll leave if you say the word."

As if it was likely she'd ask him to leave, the way her heart was acting. The way her body was turning liquid and her lips tingled. She ought to figure out which word he was talking about, but she knew she wasn't going to use it anyway.

"I'm glad you're here. Even though I ought to send you packing." Ivy frowned at him, loving the feel of his hand at her neck, the way his eyes filled with heat when he looked at her.

He was definitely slow. It took him a full minute before he pulled her the rest of the way into his arms and traced her mouth with his tongue.

"You taste of beer," she said a long while later. They were sprawled on her bunk, and he was half on top of her. His glasses were off and her robe was crumpled beneath her. The tie had come undone, and she was mostly naked. And he was taking full advantage of it.

"Sorry, I'll go brush my teeth." He pressed kisses on her throat. His hands were exploring her belly. And beyond.

Her voice was shaky. "Nope, I like beer on your breath. It's sort of decadent."

He laughed. "You've obviously led a sheltered life."

"Not all that sheltered." She dug in her bedside drawer and found the condoms she hadn't needed the night before. She slid one on him and he groaned when she used her mouth to secure it.

"That's going to do me in. Come back up here, let's make this last." He pulled her up, and his clever hands traveled down her body, fingers finding exactly where she was hot and wet and needy. She knew a rare experience when it came along, and making love with Alex was rare.

"Tell me what you want," he whispered in her ear.

You, I want you. "Surprise me," she gasped.

He paused for a long moment and then, in a smooth, deep voice, he recited, *"Under yonder beech tree, single on the green sward—"* He paused when she giggled, giving her an affronted look and then taking a nipple in his mouth, sucking hard, making her gasp.

"Be still and listen, Pierce. *Couched with her arms beneath her golden head—*" He took her wrists and trapped them above her head. She was giggling again, but there was also something wildly arousing about this.

"Knees and tresses folded, to slip and ripple idly—" He nudged her knees apart and slid slowly, excruciatingly slowly, inside her.

Ivy's laughter stopped on a sudden intake of breath. She moved against him, but he stopped her with the weight of his body.

"Lies my young love sleeping in the shade." His shaky whisper revealed the effort it took for him to finish the line. His breath came as hard as hers did. He moved in her, so slowly at first that she squirmed with frustration. And then, bodies joined, they rocked to ecstasy.

"Do you remember other poetry, or did you memorize that one just for the purposes of seduction?" Ivy felt deep contentment. Alex's leg was over her thighs, one arm under her head, the other across her breasts. There were such advantages to bunk beds and not having much space. "Not that I need variety, you can go on using the same one. Works for me. I'm just curious."

"I know lots more, and seduction had nothing to do with it. I used to recite poetry to myself when I was running. It took my mind off the pain in my lungs and legs."

"Running? As in races? Or just garden variety jogging?"

"Running. Racing."

"Do you run still?"

He nodded. "I haven't since I got here, but normally, yes. At home I run every day."

"Always have?"

"I had to learn to walk first." He gave her a tiny teasing kiss on the shoulder. "I ran a lot when I was in high school. It kept me from murdering my stepfather." He was quiet for a long moment. "That's interesting, that's the first time I've called him that without thinking about it." He repeated slowly and deliberately, "My stepfather."

"I take it you didn't get along with him?"

He snorted. "That's putting it mildly. Finding out I'm not biologically related to him is a huge relief. I pretty much spent my youth rebelling against him, or trying desperately to please him."

"And did you ever please him?"

He shrugged. "When I won races. So I ran like a maniac until I left home and went to university."

"But he must have cared about you if he adopted you. He wanted you to believe he was your father."

"Not because he cared for *me.*" There was resignation and more than a trace of bitterness in his voice. "Because he loved my mother."

Ivy felt as if she was picking at a scab. "I'm sorry."

"Don't be. I just wish it hadn't affected my relationship with my brother and sister. He never laid a hand on them. Although he was pretty much a strict, undemonstrative authority figure with all of us."

He was quiet for a long time. "I relied on scholarships and a string of part-time jobs to go away to university. My mother insisted Steve pay for the first year—one of the only times she ever confronted him."

"Did…did he lay a hand on her as well?"

"No. Just me. She used to say I provoked him." His voice grew impatient. "Don't get me wrong, Ivy, he wasn't evil. I think he just didn't know what to do with me. He certainly wasn't the father I needed. Wanted."

"I hear you." She sighed. "I always longed to have Aunt Cait for my mother. But since Dad was her brother, that whole idea was fairly incestuous."

Without looking, she knew he was smiling. "I guess nothing's ever perfect."

"This is perfect." The words were out before she could stop them. "Being here with you like this." She tensed, waiting to hear what he'd say.

"For me, too." He yawned and pressed a kiss into her hair. "You want me to go now, or can I stay?"

"Stay."

"Where have you been all my life?" He sounded groggy now.

Waiting, she wanted to say. But instead she fell asleep, cradled in his arms, comforted by his warmth.

CHAPTER FOURTEEN

It's the weirdest feeling, being somebody's father. I don't even feel like a grownup myself yet. I wonder if you do, Lindy?

From letters written by Roy Nolan,
April, 1972

THE RAIN TURNED TO SUNSHINE again, and by midweek Alex was nearly done roofing the cabins, but he'd run out of tarpaper and shingles.

Ivy had taken the copter early that morning for pipeline patrol, and Ben and the other guides were fishing with guests out on the chuck, taking advantage of the sunshine.

Alex went in search of Sage and found her in the kitchen pantry, making a list of what groceries were needed.

She turned and smiled, and once again he saw the resemblance to his former wife.

"Hey, Alex. How's the construction coming along?"

"Close to done." He explained about the tarpaper and shingles.

"We're getting dangerously low on supplies here, too. Caitlin usually stays on top of it, I should have realized sooner we were running out of staples. If I finish this list, could you take one of the boats and go to Valdez? The guides left that small crab boat behind…do you know how to run it?"

"Sure." He hadn't made the trip alone, but Bert had pointed out the obvious dangers, the places where the water was shallow and where the waves were likely to roll in hard. Alex felt confident he could manage on his own.

"I'll go clean up a little."

"Thanks." Sage turned back to the shelves and her list. "I'll be finished in about fifteen minutes. Mavis is making lunch—come and have some before you go."

After a quick shower in his cabin, Alex headed back to the kitchen.

"Here you go." Mavis plunked a bowl of chowder and a thick roast beef sandwich in front of him. She served Sage and then herself, taking a seat across from Alex. After the first week or so, she'd gotten over being self-conscious around him.

"Here's the list of supplies, and a couple of signed checks. Just don't decide to make them out for a million and head for parts unknown," Sage said with a wink.

Alex pretended to consider the possibility. "I guess I'd better leave you my backpack as collateral."

Sage laughed. “I think we’ll run on good old-fashioned trust.”

“Ivy’ll be coming back tonight,” Mavis said with a knowing glance in his direction. “He isn’t likely to cut and run as long as she’s around.”

“Collateral, big time.” Sage and Mavis giggled. They knew exactly where Alex was sleeping these nights. They teased both him and Ivy on a regular basis. He chose to ignore their pointed comments, but even though Ivy tried not to react, she couldn’t stop blushing, which delighted the two women. He found her reaction endearing and ingenuous.

“Will the stores question me, cashing checks on the lodge’s account, Sage?”

“Tell them to call me if there’s a problem. Or if Tom’s around he could vouch for you. I think he’s at the office today, Ben was talking to him earlier.”

Alex figured Tom would just as soon have him taken into custody. The man gave him a knot in his gut.

“Good soup, Mavis.” He scooped up the last spoonful and finished his sandwich. “Thanks for lunch. I’ll see you later.”

The boat trip into Valdez was spectacularly beautiful. Alex skirted the coastline, drinking in the blue of the glaciers. A bald eagle circled above him, and several hundred feet away huge shoals of silver herring stirred the water into a frenzy. Salmon circled the herring, rounding them up like cowboys, knocking them senseless with their tails and then coming back to eat them.

Alex laughed. He'd never realized fish had that much moxie. Seagulls joined in the feast, their raucous voices shrill and urgent in the clear, cold air. Farther out, a killer whale spouted.

No wonder Ivy loved this remote place, insisted that she'd never live anywhere but here. He thought of the way she curled around him each night, even in her sleep turning when he turned. She simply twined her arms around him again once he settled. She slept the way she did everything else, no careless moves, no wasted energy.

He was the one who lay awake for hours, holding her and trying not to think about where they were headed. He'd drawn the lines, and then extended them, not once, but—what? He added the nights in his head. Eight nights filled with passion.

And eight days filled with doubts, because each morning he reminded himself that he couldn't get involved—any more than he already was. But when evening came, he shoved those intentions into a lock-box and headed for Ivy's cabin.

The most frightening thing about it was that although the sex was good—*admit it, Ladrovik, the sex is over-the-top mind-blowing spectacular*—it was the company he wanted even more.

He turned the rudder to avoid a deadhead. Not

that they agreed about everything, or even about most things. She was like her father in some ways, stubborn, opinionated, certain she was right, impatient with ideas she didn't agree with. Perversely, what irritated Alex about Tom attracted and amused him in Ivy. He liked being challenged, being forced to think carefully about what he believed in. He even liked arguing with her. About most things.

The only subject that had brought them close to an out-and-out quarrel was his plan to head into the bush.

"That's not only stupid, it's foolhardy and thoughtless," Ivy had said in a derogatory tone so much like Tom's that Alex got annoyed.

"The mudflats are like quicksand," she pointed out. "We can have snowstorms right up till June that cover tracks and bodies…rivers can be streams one day and raging torrents the next. And in the spring the bears are just out of hibernation and they're hungry—have you ever even shot a rifle? I didn't think so. And you're going out alone? No offense, but you aren't exactly a lumberjack, Professor."

Her sarcasm made his hackles rise. Alex did his best to curb his irritation. "Maybe not, but before I came up here I read everything I could get my hands on about survival in the woods. I bought the best equipment. And I have a high-powered rifle." He didn't tell her that he'd only shot it a couple of times at a stationary target. "*No offense,* but I figure I can get along better in the bush than you could in the city."

Her green eyes had blazed. She wrenched herself out of bed and rooted around for her sweats. She couldn't find them soon enough. He caught her in his arms and kissed away the temper.

Since then, they'd mutually avoided that particular subject, but not talking about it didn't make it disappear. The simple fact was that soon—very soon—he was leaving. She knew it, and so did he. He also knew that leaving her wasn't going to be easy.

THE GROCERIES TOOK MUCH longer than he'd expected.

But there was no problem with the checks.

"You're that guy from down south who's building those cabins for Theo," the toothless man in the hardware store said, spraying saliva with every consonant. "Hear he's coming home in a day or two. Tell him Ned sends his best."

Two other customers added their good wishes.

The checkout woman at the grocery store said, "How's it going up at the lodge with Theo and Caitlin away? Hear he's coming home soon, tell him hey from all of us. I'm putting in a bag of those hard candies he likes."

Three other clerks and two customers chimed in with their greetings.

There were a lot of supplies. Alex made more

trips than he wanted to count down to the dock and back again loading everything in the boat. By the time he finished, it was packed to the gunwales and he needed a break, so he bought a large coffee and an even larger cinnamon bun from a little café on the waterfront and sat on a bench within view of the boat. Not that anyone would steal anything—he was convinced that the year-round residents knew everyone in town and would never dream of pilfering anything.

He was basking in the sunshine, head resting on the back of the bench, eyes closed behind his sunglasses when a woman's husky voice said, "Do you mind if I join you?"

Alex squinted up and sprang to his feet. The arrestingly beautiful woman smiling at him could've stepped from a movie screen. Even if she hadn't had her eyes, he'd have known she was Ivy's mother. How many former fashion models could one town have?

"Please, sit down." He set his coffee on the bench and wiped the sticky residue from the bun on his pant leg before offering her his hand.

"I'm Alex Ladrovik."

"Frances Pierce. Hello, Alex. I think you've met my husband, Tom, and my daughter, Ivy." Her handshake was firm. She glanced at the bench and took a folded paper towel from her handbag, fastidiously spreading it before she sat.

"These pants have to be dry cleaned," she explained.

Alex nodded. As ignorant of fashion as the next man, he did realize Frances was wearing the type of clothing women wore in San Diego to go out for lunch: high-heeled leather boots and a tailored blazer. Her thick, white hair was shoulder length and set off her sculptured cheekbones. She wore huge hoop earrings and a cluster of black and silver beads at her throat.

In this place, where the uniform seemed to be jeans or sweats and a parka, she stood out like a beacon, but he also realized her beauty would have set her apart regardless of what she wore. It was intimidating. It reduced him to the status of a stammering teen.

"Can—can I get you a coffee? Maybe a cinnamon bun?"

Her smile was a benediction. "Yes, please, I'd like that."

Alex was back in a few moments. Frances thanked him and bit hungrily into the bun.

"Mmm, that's delicious," she murmured. "You've probably guessed this meeting wasn't exactly accidental. I saw you in the grocery store and followed you here." She sipped at her coffee. "I heard that you and Ivy were—are—friends. There really aren't any secrets in a small town, you see. And I wanted to meet you."

Alex smiled. "I've wanted to meet you, too. But

Ivy and I—well, we haven't really had much time—we haven't known each other very long..." Did she know that he was with Ivy every night, all night?

She put a hand on his arm. "No excuses necessary, Alex." Her smile faded. "Ivy and I—" Her breath caught and she put a hand to her throat. "She—she finds me difficult. With good reason. We don't see one another that often."

"I'm sorry." He couldn't think what else to say.

"So am I." She looked out over the harbor. "The problem is with me, not her. It always has been. I'm hopeless at mothering, I know that." Her smile was infinitely sad this time, and unshed tears glinted in her eyes. "Good thing I only have Ivy to ruin. Think if I'd had six kids, the damage I might have done."

Alex felt sorry for her, and he didn't stop to edit his response. "She told me you also had a son who died."

Frances looked surprised. "Yes, I did. *We* did," she corrected. "I didn't know that Ivy thought about Jacob much anymore. It was a very long time ago, and he was two years older than Ivy. She was just a toddler at the time."

"She told me. My daughter died, too. My Annie." It still hurt him to say her name. "She was three. It...it changed me." He suddenly felt inexplicably close to this woman. He felt she understood.

He was right, because she drew her breath in

sharply and then took his hand. She held it firmly for a long moment before she gave it a final squeeze and released it.

"Losing Jacob changed me, as well," she said on a long sigh. "I think—" she gave her head a vehement shake, silver hair rippling around her face "—I *know,* that in some way it stopped me from being as close to Ivy as I might have been. I was scared of losing her as well, so I didn't let myself get close. Do you know what I mean?"

"Yes, I do." Her words seemed to echo in his head. "I quit my job. I got divorced, came to Alaska."

"At least you did something." Her voice was sad, and when she didn't say anything further, they sat in companionable silence.

She drank the rest of her coffee, which must have been cold by now. The remainder of the cinnamon bun sat on the napkin beside her.

"When I followed you here, I didn't know exactly what I wanted to say to you, Alex. I think I just needed to know that you were a decent man. I had no idea...that I'd feel so comfortable with you." She flashed him a mischievous smile. "We have Ivy in common, of course. Even an arm's-length mother worries about the man her daughter's seriously involved with."

He felt a stab of panic then, because obviously people were talking about him and Ivy. And Frances had the wrong slant on their relationship. She needed to understand that it wasn't either long-term or serious. He was trying to find a diplomatic way of saying that when she added, "And of course Tom is doing the typical father thing, getting all bristly and protective."

Tom was all of that, all right. "I don't know what Tom's told you about me," Alex began hesitantly. He was going to have to be very cautious here.

He was planning his next words when Frances said, "Nothing, really, except that Ivy's in love with you."

CHAPTER FIFTEEN

The weather's warm, the sun is shining and I'm writing this while having lousy coffee in a greasy spoon down by the harbor.

From letters written by Roy Nolan,
April, 1972

ALEX COULDN'T SPEAK. He could barely breathe.

Frances didn't seem to notice. She wasn't watching him. Her eyes were on the water as she said, "You see, Tom and I are…I guess the word's estranged. The only thing we really have in common anymore is Ivy."

"Then why…why do you stay together?" He hardly knew what he was saying, except that it was so much safer to keep the conversation on Frances.

Ivy's in love with you.

She shrugged. "Fear. For years I've believed I was far too old to do the work I was best at. When I finally started feeling better, I played at teaching, did volunteer work. But recently, I've found out there are new opportunities for me, thanks to the aging baby boomers."

"In modeling?" His mouth was on automatic pilot.

"I guess Ivy told you?"

"Yes, she did."

"It was a very long time ago. In another lifetime. But maybe—"

She got abruptly to her feet, picked up the cinnamon bun and dropped it in a nearby garbage bin. Wiping her fingers on a tissue, she picked up her handbag. "I must go. It's been good to meet you, Alex."

"And you." He still felt dazed.

She was about to walk away, and then her amazing eyes looked straight into his.

"You're going to tell Ivy we met."

"Yes, of course."

She gave him a pleading look. "I can't tell you what to do, but I'd be grateful if you didn't tell her what I said. The part about her loving you? She'd think I was meddling in her private business." Frances sighed. "She'd be right. It's just, well, what can I say? I'm her mother."

"I understand. I'll treat it as a confidence."

"Thanks." She flashed him a smile that could still have graced the cover of any magazine, and then she was gone. She had a distinctive walk, bold and attention-grabbing, and tourists and locals alike turned to watch at her as she made her way down the street. She turned a corner and disappeared.

It felt as if Alex had been punched in the gut. Now

that it was too late, he realized there were questions he should have asked—like how did Tom know? Had Ivy confided in her father, told him she was in love with Alex? Or did Tom just assume so because he'd heard they were sleeping together?

Sex was one thing, but love? He couldn't deal with love. He was going to have to break it off, the sooner the better.

He had very little left to do on the cabins, a bit of roofing, it wouldn't take long once he had the shingles. There was finishing work still to be done, but that had to wait until an electrician came to do the wiring. The rough plumbing was in place, but again, there was nothing more Alex could do until a plumber put in a septic field. His job was ending. The weather was growing warmer as each day lengthened. It was time for him to do what he'd come here for.

He headed down to the boat and cast off, but the trip back held none of the magic or the lightheartedness he'd felt on his way into town that morning.

Oliver was down at the dock when he arrived, unloading fishing gear from one of the Boston whalers. He grabbed the line Alex tossed him. "Great news," he said with a wide smile. "Theo and Caitlin got home. Ivy brought them in the copter."

Alex looked over at the landing pad, but it was empty.

"She had to take off again right away," Oliver explained. "She had a last-minute booking for a scenic tour from some oil magnates from Texas."

It was a relief not to have to face her yet. "How's Theo looking?"

"Not bad, considering. He's lost a lot of weight, and he's pasty from being in the hospital so long, but he's moving pretty good."

Together, they hauled tarpaper and shingles to the shed and boxes of groceries up to the kitchen, where Caitlin was standing at the stove, browning onions in a huge pan.

"Alex." She set her spoon down, turned the stove off and came hurrying over to greet him. She took both his hands in hers.

"I want you to know how grateful Theo and I are for everything you've done while we were gone. Ben and Sage said they couldn't have managed here without you."

"They're exaggerating, but thank you."

"Come through to the den and say hi to Theo. He's delighted to be home. And so am I."

"Not half as glad as I am," Mavis said in an acerbic tone. "One more week trying to run this kitchen on my own and I'd have headed for the bush."

Caitlin patted the other woman's shoulder. "From what the guests told me about your wonderful meals, they might just not want me back."

Mavis gave a snort that managed to sound both doubtful and delighted.

Caitlin took Alex's arm and led him down the hall to the den where Theo was sitting in a recliner. He got up when they came in.

"I told this young man you'd want to see him and thank him yourself, dearest," Caitlin said. The love she felt for her husband was obvious in her voice. It made Alex suddenly feel lonely.

"I sure do." Theo was much thinner and older-looking. There was a fragility about him that shocked Alex as he took the older man's hand.

"Welcome home, Theo. It's very good to have you back."

"Thank you. Ben said you did everything but dust while I was taking it easy in that hospital bed. I want you to know how grateful I am, son. And I saw the cabins when we landed—they look wonderful. I haven't had a chance to take a closer look yet, but it was a real pleasure to see them so nearly completed." Theo sank back into the recliner and gestured at an easy chair beside him. "Sit down, tell me what's left to do on them."

Alex gave him a brief summary, and they discussed plumbing and electricity. Then Alex said, "There's only a couple of hours work left. When I have the roofs finished, Theo, I'm going to be leaving."

Theo nodded. "I figured as much. You've already

done way more than we agreed to in the beginning. Just let me know when you plan to head off, and I'll have a check for you."

"Thanks. It'll probably be in the next day or two."

"Heading off into the bush, like you planned?"

"Yes." Again, Alex had that sinking feeling in his gut. "The weather's good, I'd like to get started."

"Any chance you might want a full-time job when your trek is over? We could use a man with your diverse talents around here."

Alex shook his head. "Thank you, Theo. The offer's much appreciated. But I think I'll be going back when my trip is over."

"Our loss. Before you set off into the bush, you be sure to leave us a detailed map. For safety's sake."

"I will. I've really enjoyed my time here at the lodge. I only wish you hadn't been sick."

"Me, too, son. Me, too."

Theo seemed to be fading, so Alex got to his feet. "I've left Oliver unloading the boat. He won't be very impressed with me unless I get back out there."

"I'll see you at supper, then." With an exhausted smile, Theo used the controls to tip the chair back and, by the time Alex left the room, the older man's eyes were closed.

Outside, the day was clouding over and the wind off the ocean was brisk. Alex shivered, but the cold he felt had nothing to do with the weather. He glanced over at the empty helipad. He'd told Theo. Now he'd have to tell Ivy he was leaving, and the thought filled him with dread.

IVY LANDED THE COPTER, relieved beyond belief to be back at the office. Rick and Irv, the two men she'd spent the afternoon flying around, were easily the most objectionable idiots she'd ever met. They'd made one crude sexual joke after the other, and they'd each taken a turn at trying to convince her to spend the evening with them. Most damning of all from Ivy's point of view, they'd been totally oblivious to the raw beauty of the country she'd flown them over.

"End of the line, gentlemen, everybody out." *Gentlemen* was her private sarcasm, and her smile was more like a grimace, but these two idiots were too self-absorbed and thick-skulled to even notice.

"Honey, you sure you won't change your mind about tonight? We'll show you the best time this burg has to offer. Money's no object. We got unlimited expense accounts, right, Irv?"

"Righty-o. And it would be real sweet of you to line up a friend, honey. Maybe one of those little native girls prancing around in tight jeans," Irv the nerd added.

"The answer's still no." Ivy didn't care if she sounded rude. All she wanted was to get these two gone and go into the office bathroom to wash.

As soon as they were out of the copter, she turned on her heel and made for the trailer. She could hear them behind her, arguing now over whether it was possible to even get a decent piece of tail in this godforsaken hick town. Fuming, she felt like going back and kicking them in the balls, but she settled for slamming the trailer door as hard as she could—and was amazed to find her mother and father sitting in the office.

Tom was behind the desk, and Frances was seated in the old wooden armchair across from him. There was a large brown envelope and several legal-looking documents in front of Tom.

They turned toward her, and she instantly sensed the tension in the atmosphere.

"Bad trip?" Tom squinted out the window at the two paunchy men now sauntering down the street.

"Bad as it gets. I charged them double the usual rate—I should have tripled it." She nodded at Frances. "Hi, Mom. I have to use the bathroom, be out in a sec."

She took her time washing, trying to imagine what was going on. Frances hardly ever dropped by the office. Ivy walked out and poured herself a coffee, noting that both her parents had full mugs that looked untouched.

"So what's up, guys?" She tried for a casual tone, but she was beginning to feel anxious.

Frances glanced at Tom, but he shook his head and shrugged. When she spoke, Frances's voice was higher-pitched than normal.

"Tom and I are separating, Ivy. I've brought your father the legal papers to sign. I'll be moving to New York as soon as the school year ends. I have an offer of a job there."

It shouldn't have been such a huge shock. Ivy had always known their marriage wasn't the stuff romance novels were made of. In high school, when her best friend's parents were going through a bitter divorce, Ivy had been certain it would happen to her parents as well. But the years passed, and they seemed to arrive at some sort of agreement. She'd gotten lulled into believing they'd stay together forever.

Frances was watching her. Ivy hadn't noticed before that there were lines around her mother's mouth and eyes. "I wanted to tell you that day we had lunch, Ivy, but you left before I could."

"So what were you planning to do, Mom, leave me a little note the day you left?" That was sarcastic, but Ivy couldn't help herself.

"I—I was hoping—" Her mother looked over at Tom. "I know you're close to your father, I was hoping he'd explain."

"That would suit you fine, wouldn't it, *Mother?*" She was shaking. Ivy set the mug she was holding down on the table. The coffee slopped over the rim. It had dripped all over her shirt.

"Just like always, you'd leave it up to Dad to clean up your mess."

She grabbed a towel and gave the stains a vicious rub. "You wouldn't have to get into any nasty emotional stuff that way, would you?"

"Ivy, please—" Frances got up and came over. She put a hand out, but Ivy brushed it away. She felt like striking her mother.

"How can you do this? I mean, it's really not such a big deal for me, but how can you treat Dad this way? He loves you, you know that. He's the one who's always been there for you, he's the one who picked up the slack when I was little and you were depressed all the time." Ivy's voice rose. "If you were so dissatisfied, why didn't you leave years ago? Why wait till now?"

Frances kept her voice soft and even. "Because I was sick, Ivy. Depression is an illness, like any other."

"That's it? You were depressed and now you're not, so now you can walk away?"

"That's not how it is at all." Frances put her jacket on and picked up her handbag. She gathered up the legal papers and fitted them back into their envelope. "Ivy, I hope we can talk when you're not so angry."

"Yeah, well, don't hold your breath."

Frances left without another word.

Ivy waited until the door closed after her and then sank into the chair where her mother had been sitting.

"I suppose she wants half of everything you've got," she raged. "Which will affect the business, right? You'll have to mortgage Up And Away in order to pay her off, won't you, Dad?"

"That's between your mother and me."

She could hear in Tom's voice how upset he was.

"It won't affect your share of the business, we agreed on that. You shouldn't be so hard on her, honey."

Disgusted, Ivy sprang to her feet again. "How can you say that? You always defend her, Dad." She strode up and down the small area. "Maybe I should look on the bright side, maybe you'll be better off without her."

"Don't ever say such a thing." Teeth clenched, Tom got up and put his jacket on. "I don't want to hear any more about it. I'm taking Bert up for a lesson, he'll be along any minute. Are you taking the copter back to the lodge tonight?"

For a moment, her anger flared at her father as well. In his way, he was as bad as Frances at avoidance.

"I've got a booking with those German people for early tomorrow morning. They want to see where the eagles are nesting."

"I probably won't see you until tomorrow afternoon, then." He hesitated. "Do me a favor and don't mention anything about this at the lodge. I'll tell them when I'm ready."

"I won't say anything." She wouldn't have told Caitlin even if he hadn't asked; there was always that hint of discord between her aunt and her mother. And even now, as furious as she was with Frances, Ivy still wouldn't betray her mother that way.

"Thanks." He sighed and put an arm around her shoulders, squeezing her for a moment. "Don't take it so hard, Ivy. I've known it was coming for a long time."

He was out the door before she could reply.

Feeling deserted, she drew in a sobbing breath, realizing she was close to tears. There was only one cure when she felt this upset. She needed to fly.

She watched from the window until her father and Bert motored out into the chuck and took off, and then she went out to the copter, forcing herself to concentrate on the preflight checks, the procedure for liftoff.

As the Bell rose into the afternoon sky and the little town of Valdez melded into the surrounding mountainous landscape, Ivy waited for her mood to improve. But it didn't happen. Then, in a short time, the lodge came into view and, as she guided the copter down, she saw Alex.

He was walking in the direction of his cabin, and he looked up and waved. The sight of him finally lifted her spirits.

Once the copter was safely on the landing pad, it came to her that she wanted nothing more than to be with Alex. She wanted him to hold her close as she told him about her parents. She could confide in him. She felt safe and secure when she was with him. Even though they argued sometimes, she respected his opinion.

Sitting behind the controls, she could see her little cabin, although Alex's was hidden, shielded by a grove of trees. She wondered for a moment why he hadn't come over when he'd seen she was about to land.

She didn't dwell on it. There were enough troubling things to think about, including the fact that there was now no reason for her to be staying here. She'd have to pack up her gear and move back to town, which meant she wouldn't be able to spend every night with Alex anymore.

That fact just plummeted her back into her earlier darkness.

On so many different levels, she was involved with him. She was strong enough to handle this emotional stuff on her own, she knew that. She just didn't want to. She wanted Alex's input, his support, his viewpoint. She wanted him.

This thing with Alex *was* different. This time, the more they were together, the more time she wanted to spend with him.

He made her laugh, he made her think, he made her angry and then kissed and teased her out of it again.

Her heart slammed into her ribs as she admitted

to herself that she was in love with him. Should she tell him? She shook her head. Now wasn't the time.

There were other things she needed to tell him. She climbed out of the copter and headed for his cabin. "Knock, knock, anybody home?" She opened the door, trying to sound upbeat.

Alex was standing at the window, looking out at the ocean. He didn't say anything as she stripped off her jacket and her boots.

She walked over and wrapped her arms around him, breathing in his familiar smell. His arms came up and held her close, and for the first time in hours she felt safe.

"Professor, I'm so glad you're here. I really need to talk to you."

"Okay." He kissed her softly, released her and moved to the table. He pulled out a chair for her and took the one opposite. "I'm listening."

Ivy sat down, wishing he'd gone on holding her. But the cabin was too small for a couch, and the bunk was the only other alternative. Actually, it was the one she'd have chosen.

He reached across and took her hand in his, interlacing their fingers so their palms were joined. "You go first."

She was too consumed by her own troubled emotions to notice how serious he was being.

"My mother's leaving," she burst out. "She's divorcing my dad, leaving Valdez, moving to New York. I just found out."

There was a long silence. She watched his face and waited for him to say something.

"Maybe she's doing what she needs to do, Ivy."

"Oh, I'm sure she thinks so." Her bitterness and anger spilled out in a flood of words. "She's so goddamned *selfish.* All my father and I have ever done is pay attention to what Frances needs. The whole household always revolved around her. Dad and I would tiptoe around when she was having one of her low times, which was every other week. We'd bend over backward trying to please her, but she never appreciated anything. And now when she's finally on some sort of an even keel, well, now she's walking out on him."

Again, he was silent for quite a long time. He blew out a breath and then said, "Marriage is never all one-sided, Ivy. No one ever knows what's really between two people."

"*I* know." She banged their joined hands on the table for emphasis. "I lived with them, remember?" It irritated her that he wasn't sympathizing. "I know you and Dad have some issues, but believe me, if you'd ever met my mother, you'd realize that the problems in their marriage aren't his fault. Not by a long shot."

He waited a heartbeat, and then he said, "I did meet your mother, Ivy. I liked her very much."

CHAPTER SIXTEEN

I can't wait much longer for the weather to get better, money just evaporates hanging around Valdez. Hope all's well with you and the sprout.

From letters written by Roy Nolan,
April, 1972

IVY FROWNED. "You—what? You met Frances?" She stared at him, astounded. "When? How could you meet her? She never comes here."

"I met her today, in Valdez. I had to take a boat and go into town for supplies. She stopped and introduced herself. We talked for a while."

"Talked? With *Frances?* About what?" An entire new sense of betrayal was beginning to take form and her gut reacted, cramping.

"About your brother, Jacob. About Annie. Losing them gave us something in common."

"She talked about Jacob? She never talks about Jacob." Not to Ivy, anyway. "What time was this?" She hugged her belly. She needed to know exactly when.

"About three."

"Three. So, did she happen to mention she was heading over to the office right then to get Dad to sign separation papers?"

"Of course not. She wouldn't tell me something like that." He was losing patience with her. And he was defending her mother, which hurt like hell.

He seemed distracted, and Ivy began to sense that there was something more, something he wasn't saying. His voice was gentle and even that angered her. She pulled her hand away as he went on in a perfectly maddening, reasonable voice.

"I've heard that when your parents divorce, it's traumatic, no matter what age you are, Ivy. But don't you think you're reacting a little too strongly here? You do have a tendency to worship your father, and maybe that's clouding your judgment just a little about Frances." He stopped and frowned. "Sorry. That's such a load of pop psychology it's nauseating." He reached over to take her hand again, but she snatched it away. "Come on, Ivy. Don't be so hard on her. Nobody's perfect."

Her voice rose. "Don't you think I know that? I do know both of them, they're my parents, for God's sake. And I don't think you have the right to make judgments. You've only met my mother once. That's hardly enough time to find out what she's really like."

"I agree, that's true." His tone became stubborn. "But I found her a lot easier to get on with than Tom."

"Really? I don't suppose the fact that she's drop-dead gorgeous had anything to do with that." She knew that was way out of line, but she didn't care. "Men have been known to lose the power of speech around my mother."

Instead of getting defensive, he just looked amused. "Now you're really being childish."

She knew that, too. And she certainly didn't appreciate having him remind her. She was close to tears again. She'd come to him for comfort.

"I should go." She started to get to her feet.

"Wait, please. There's something I need to tell you."

She sank back into the chair. "Okay, I'm listening."

"The cabins are nearly done. There's still a little carpentry after the electricity and plumbing go in, but Ben can easily manage that."

"You're leaving." The bottom seemed to drop out of her stomach.

"Yes. I told Theo this afternoon."

"When? When are you going?" As if it mattered.

"Tomorrow, probably." He leaned toward her. "Ivy, you know I came up here to follow my father's map. I need to find out what I can about him, and this is the only way that feels right to me."

"Are you coming back?" She hated herself for even asking.

"My Jeep is in Valdez." His words came out faster, defensive. "But I won't be staying long. I have to get back to San Diego, pick up the pieces of my life. I'll be in touch. I'll certainly see you when I get back, but it may not be for more than a day or two."

How revealing that he'd come back to reclaim, not her, but his damned vehicle. She would not, could not, let him see how deeply he'd hurt her. She couldn't smile, but she didn't cry, either. She was proud of herself for that.

"Well, then, I guess this is goodbye, Alex. I hope you find whatever it is you're looking for. And that you get back safe from your expedition." The tears she'd been holding back unexpectedly caught up with her, and she bolted for the door.

He intercepted her. He put his arms around her and held her tight. She fought him at first, but he held on.

"Ivy, sweetheart, please don't cry," he pleaded. "And don't leave me this way, either. Don't go rushing off before we really talk about it."

She couldn't speak. She shook her head and struggled, but his arms only tightened. "I keep wishing I'd met you under different circumstances, at a different time in my life," he whispered. "I care about you, Ivy." He drew a deep, shuddering breath. "I've loved being with you. You are so beautiful, in every way. I've never known a woman as strong and independent as you are."

Big deal. He was leaving anyway. She sniffed and tried for control, without too much luck. "Don't... don't give me that, Ladrovik. You were married to a cop, remember?" And being called strong and independent would have been funny if she wasn't so miserable.

She felt needy and miserable, and she hated feeling this way. She hated him for making her feel this way. Except she didn't. She loved him, and she hated that, too.

"I can't promise you a damned thing," he said, and now it was Alex who sounded angry.

"Did—" Her throat closed. She swallowed and tried again. "Did I ever ask for promises?"

He didn't answer. She'd never felt as desperately lonely as she did right at this moment, held so tight and close she could feel his heart hammering behind his rib cage.

She finally stepped back, out of his embrace. She had to salvage her pride, and if she stayed any longer she'd break down completely and do something horrible. Like beg. "I need to be alone for a while."

"I'll see you later up at the lodge?"

"Sure." The lie was the only thing that came easy as she headed blindly out the door.

ALEX TOOK A FEW STEPS after her, and then stopped. He knew he'd totally screwed up, but going after her now wouldn't change anything, so what was the point? All the talking in the world wasn't going to alter the outcome. It wasn't as if he'd misled her. He'd been clear from the very beginning about what he was offering, and it sure as hell hadn't been much.

You never even took her on a proper date, Ladrovik. They'd both been way too busy, trying to keep ahead of things at the lodge. But he still wished they'd gone out somewhere, watched a movie, maybe danced a little. He could have borrowed a boat, taken her into town for a few hours.

Instead, all they'd done was talk and argue and laugh and make love, mostly in this cabin. On that bunk. A sick emptiness filled him when he thought about the loss of those nights, listening to her voice in the twilight, the smell of wood burning in the heater mixed with the tang of her eucalyptus soap. Her soft, steady breathing as she slept, curled up against him in the narrow bunk.

But damn it all, it wasn't his fault she'd fallen in love with him. It sure as hell wasn't something he'd set out to accomplish. And right there was the real source of the anguish he felt, painful and acute.

He'd never had to try with Ivy. Being with her was the most natural, easygoing, comfortable relationship he'd ever had. Which was exactly why he had to leave now, before…

He was sweating, and the stove wasn't even lit. He

scrabbled through the drawer, looking for the running shorts and singlet he hadn't used since coming to Valdez. Everyone had told him that running in the woods was dangerous, that the bears were coming out of hibernation, hungry and short-tempered.

Bears, hell. He'd take his chances with bears over these feelings any day. He pulled his runners on and hurriedly laced them. He had to move, run, get this tightness out of his chest, get Ivy out of his mind.

He went out the cabin door and headed for the rutted path that angled up the mountain. At first, it was tough, because he hadn't run for weeks. It took a while to find the rhythm, the stride that would carry him long distances with minimal effort. Once he found it, Alex concentrated on breathing, on the movement of his arms, on the roughness of the terrain.

It took a long time, and sweat was pouring off him before he decided that he wasn't thinking of Ivy at all.

CHAPTER SEVENTEEN

See you in August, Lindy. September at the latest.
From letters written by Roy Nolan,
April, 1972

"WELL, THAT'S OVER. Alex just dumped me." Ivy was over her tears and into outrage by the time she got to Sage's house.

Her friend was behind the computer, probably trying to catch up on the bookkeeping that she'd had to ignore for the past several weeks.

"He *what?*" Sage flew over and wrapped her arms around Ivy. "Oh, sweetie, why? Did you guys have a fight?"

"It wasn't that." Her voice was shaking, and Ivy didn't even try to control it. "He's leaving tomorrow to walk off into the stupid bush, and he made it plain that if and when he gets back, he's heading straight south. After he picks up his beloved Jeep, of course. Oh, yeah, and if he can fit me in, he'll come by and say hi. And he'll be in touch. He made sure not to give me a phone number or anywhere I could reach him."

Sage's eyes were wide, disbelief in her expression. "He didn't really say that."

"Yeah, he did. Words to that effect, anyhow."

Sage was outraged. "The lowlife. The rat. Did you kick him hard in a vulnerable spot?" She took Ivy's hand. "C'mon, I've got a big bar of dark chocolate and a quart of ice cream, let's go down and indulge."

Ivy shook her head. "Thanks, but I can't. I feel sick. I'm going to skip supper."

"Are you going flying?" Sage knew her so well.

Ivy shook her head. "With the price of gas, it's just not practical to take the chopper back into town when I've got to pick up guests here in the morning. Oliver's heading into Valdez in a boat with a couple of the tourists. They want to experience the local night life. I'm going with them. I really don't want to have to see Alex again tonight."

"That I can understand. Want me to tell Caitlin for you?"

"Oh, Sage, would you? I just can't face telling Aunt Cait, not when this is Theo's first night home. She'll want to know why and, honestly, Sage, I just can't get into it."

"No problem, hon. I'll tell her for you. Is that big blond German guy going with Oliver?"

"Hans? Probably."

"Good." Sage's eyes narrowed. "I'll just accidentally let Alex know that."

"I doubt he'll even ask. He's got other, more important things on his mind."

"Oh, yeah? I wouldn't bet on it. I've seen the way he looks at you. And everybody's noticed that dazed and stupefied expression on his face at breakfast every morning."

"Everybody?" Ivy felt the color rise in her cheeks. "You and Mavis, yeah, but *everybody?*"

"No secrets in this goldfish bowl."

"Oh, geez. And now they'll all know he dumped me."

"Nope, because I'll let it slip it's the other way round. And between you and me, Ivy, I wouldn't write him off quite yet. Sometimes guys take a while to figure out what it is they really want, they're kind of backward that way."

"And I'm supposed to sit and wait while he mulls it over? I don't think so. Ben didn't ever do that to you, did he?"

"No, he didn't. We were on the same page, at least in the beginning." There was a wistful note in Sage's voice.

"And you're not now?"

Sage hesitated. "We're okay, we're just going through a rough patch. Every couple hits those now and then."

Like Ivy's mother and father. She'd tell Sage about them, but not right now. One thing at a time.

"Ben and I'll get through it," Sage said. "Just like you'll get over this."

"God, I really hope so. Thanks for being such a great friend, Sage."

"It works both ways."

Ivy was trying not to cry again. "I'd better get down to the dock, Oliver's liable to take off without me. Tell Aunt Cait I'll get Dad to drop me back here early tomorrow morning so I can do the tour."

"I will." Sage grabbed Ivy's hand and gave it a squeeze. "Have fun tonight. Put Ladrovik right out of your head."

"I intend to." And she'd have a good time as well, Ivy resolved, as she hurried down to the dock. It had been a while since she'd gone out to dinner. It had been a while since she'd gone out anywhere, come to think of it.

The German tourists—particularly Hans—were delighted when she agreed to join them at the Pipeline Club. Besides having great steaks and a half-decent lounge, they wanted to view for themselves the watering hole where Captain Hazelwood had his famous last drink before running the Exxon-Valdez aground.

It wasn't Ivy's favorite place. Like most of Valdez's natives, she was sick of hearing anything about Hazelwood. But tonight was a case of any port in a storm. She only half listened to their cheerful chatter as the boat slid through the water. Her mind was like a treadmill, going from her parents to Alex and back again.

"I need to change, see you in an hour," she promised when the boat docked at the Valdez wharf. She set off on foot and was fitting her key into the lock on her home in less than fifteen minutes.

Her little house was warm and quiet. Normally, it gave her a sense of pride and peace to be herc, in the home she'd created for herself, but today nothing felt right. She showered quickly, and without giving it much thought, pulled on a pair of black slacks and a white cashmere sweater from her bottom drawer. Jamming into her good cowboy boots and, with a gold chain Tom had given her for her twenty-first birthday, she grabbed her suede jacket and truck keys and locked the door after herself. By moving fast, she was sure she could put her mind on hold.

She stopped by the office to tell Tom she needed a lift to the lodge in the morning, and was relieved when he wasn't there. She left a note on Kisha's desk for him and headed for the Pipeline Club.

The tourists were already on their second or third pre-dinner drink. They made a great show of ordering her two cocktails so she'd catch up, and Ivy drank them quickly.

But instead of numbing anything, the liquor made her feel worse about everything. They moved to the dining room and everyone ordered the steak that the Pipeline was famous for. Ivy cut it up and messed it around, but her stomach revolted at the idea of actually eating anything.

There was a live band, country and western, and when the dinner plates were cleared away Hans bowed to her and held out a hand.

"Would you dance with me, Ivy?"

"Why not?" Ivy slipped into his arms. He was tall, taller than Alex.

The song was a sad one, an old country ballad about lost love. Hans was solid, big and handsome in a typically blond, Germanic way. He was a good dancer, not madly inventive, but rhythmic. From the dinner conversation she knew he was also intelligent enough—he was a financier of some kind. He even might be sexy, if she could get her mind off Alex long enough to want to find out.

"I would like to take you somewhere else, somewhere quiet, just the two of us," he said in her ear. "You are such a beautiful woman, Ivy. I want to know you better."

"Thank you." She could invite him home with her. She could take him to bed. Sex would distract her, keep her from thinking.

Except that it wouldn't. The song came to an end,

and she extricated herself from his arms and gave Hans what she hoped was a smile.

"I'm going to have to go now," she told him. "There's something I absolutely have to do." Over everyone's protests, Ivy put money on the table to cover her share of the bill. She pulled on her jacket and headed for the door.

She'd thought she needed people and distraction, but what she really wanted was to be alone. Trying to stop herself from thinking about Alex was like the old joke about telling someone not to think about the Eiffel Tower.

She was halfway home, passing her parents' house, before she remembered that her father and mother were getting divorced. She couldn't believe she'd forgotten. She still felt rotten about it, but not as bad as she had earlier that day, before Alex gave her his prepared speech.

It was amazing that what had seemed devastating to her that afternoon had now taken a back seat to something even worse. She turned the corner onto her street. Her father's truck was in front of her house, and the lights were on in her kitchen. Ivy pulled up behind the other vehicle and sat for a moment before getting out.

For the first time in her life, she absolutely didn't want to see Tom. He'd never liked Alex, and although tonight she didn't much like him herself, she still didn't want to listen to Tom telling her she was better off without him. How perverse was that?

Slowly, she made her way inside.

Her father had made coffee. Ivy could smell it the moment she came in the door.

"Hi, Dad." She couldn't take it out on him; he was as much a victim here as she was. He probably needed company tonight.

She smiled. "I could sure use a cup of that."

Tom poured her a mug and sat across from her at the table.

"I need to talk to you, Ivy."

If one more person said that to her today, she was going to scream. "Does it have to be tonight?"

"I figure it does. It's about your mother and me."

"Look, Dad, you don't have to explain anything. I understand, honest." She wanted a bath. She wanted to go to bed. She wanted to be alone. Why was that so difficult to accomplish? "Let's not talk about it anymore tonight, okay? I know how you feel." Better than he realized.

Tom shook his head. "You don't know, Ivy." His work-worn hands were laced tight around the coffee cup, one on top of the other, and his knuckles were white. "I can't let you go on blaming your mother for everything that's wrong between us."

"Yeah? Well, that's chivalrous of you, but I know

her, remember?" Ivy's tone was sharp because she was fast losing what little patience she had left.

Tom cleared his throat. "I made mistakes, Ivy, and there's no going back."

"Everyone makes mistakes." She stirred sugar into her coffee, praying it would give her the energy to get through this. "Please, Dad, can't we talk about something else? I'm sick of going over this, and I'm really tired. I need to go to bed." She shoved the coffee away. What was she thinking, caffeine and sugar when she probably wasn't going to be able to sleep anyway?

"I had an affair." Tom's voice was shaking. "With Mavis. After Jacob died."

It took a moment for the unbelievable words to really sink in.

"With *Mavis?*" She was too stunned to even feel anything. She was numb. For some time, she couldn't even speak. Finally, she croaked, "You—you and—and Mavis?"

He couldn't look her in the eye. He nodded, head down, so she could see the bald spot on the crown of his head. "Yeah. See, we knew each other all our lives, long before I ever met your mother. Mavis was a good friend of Cait's. They worked together at the hotel. She was a cute little thing…one thing led to another. There was an understanding between us that we'd get married someday. Then when I met Frances—" He shrugged and held out his hands, palms up.

Ivy said in a whisper, "You dumped Mavis. For Mom." Things she'd never understood slowly began to fall into place. The fact that Frances didn't go to the lodge—maybe it wasn't because she was jealous of Ivy's relationship with Caitlin, as Ivy'd always believed. Maybe it was because Mavis was there.

"Yeah." Tom rubbed a weary hand across his face. "And then when we lost Jacob—I went a little nuts. More than a little. Frances was lost in a world of her own, I couldn't reach her. I needed someone to talk to, and Mavis was there. I never intended to…I never thought I'd…but I was so lonely, Ivy. So bloody alone and lonely." He sounded miserable and ordinarily, she'd have tripped over her feet rushing to his defense.

Not now. She was trying to take it in, to make sense of it. Her mother had always seemed difficult and temperamental.

Against her will, she began to imagine a woman who'd lost a child, who needed her husband perhaps more than she ever had—and was betrayed instead.

Her father had turned to another woman. To Mavis. It was unbelievable. If anyone else had told Ivy this, she'd have called them a liar. Or laughed.

She got up for a glass of water. Her hands were shaking. She took a gulp. With her back to her father, she said, "How—how long did it go on? With Mavis?"

"About a year."

Ivy was shocked a second time. Weeks, she could maybe understand. Months, perhaps. But a *year?*

She turned around and gave him a scathing look. "How could you, Dad? How could you do such a rotten thing?"

Tom's face was magenta. She could see the shame in his eyes. "I can't explain it, Ivy. I won't make excuses—there aren't any to make. Frances found out and she's never been able to forgive me. She changed after that."

"No kidding." For the first time in her life, Ivy put herself in her mother's place. "That's when she got sick, right? That's when the depression started?"

Tom shook his head. "No. It started with Jacob. But this sure didn't help."

"Why—why didn't Mom ever tell me any of this?" But of course she could guess.

Frances would never tell her daughter something shameful like this. *Not about Tom. Not when Ivy idolized him.* Her mother had never in any way tried to interfere with that relationship.

Not when Ivy idolized him. Coming on top of everything else, this was more than Ivy thought she could bear. She felt physically ill, on the verge of vomiting. "I want you to go now, please."

"Ivy—" Tom got up and came toward her.

"No." She held up a hand like a traffic cop, warning him off. "I don't want to be around you right now."

His shoulders slumped. "Honey, I'd do anything

in my power to change the past." His voice was despondent. "But I can't. I have to live with it, and it eats away at me every single day. I love Frances, I always will. I'm losing her, I deserve that, but I don't want to lose you, too. I love you, honey, more than I can say."

She knew he was begging for forgiveness. She knew he was waiting for her to say that she loved him, too.

Of course, she did love him. But right at this moment, she didn't respect him, and that was ripping her apart inside. She'd never dreamed him capable of anything like this. And like a ship hitting the tip of an iceberg, some of the things she'd thought about her mother all these years were beginning to tear through her consciousness. She'd been unkind to Frances, not overtly, perhaps, but certainly in her thoughts.

And in her actions as well, she admitted.

She'd judged her mother in so many ways, not just once, but uncountable times over the years.

To his credit, Tom had always defended Frances. But he'd never explained any of this to Ivy. Maybe when she was a teenager, it wouldn't have been appropriate, but she'd been an adult for a long time.

When she didn't say anything, Tom took his jacket and cap from the hooks by the door.

"You still want a lift out to the lodge in the morning?" His voice was subdued.

It was an effort to have to think about tourists and

schedules. She tried to focus. “Yes, I do. I should leave here about seven.”

“I’ll have the plane ready when you get to the office. See you in the morning,” he said as he went out the door.

She went over and locked the door behind him, then slumped over, resting her head against the wood. What now? In the space of a few hours, her world had been turned upside down. She felt as if every ounce of energy had been sucked out of her. She wanted to crawl into bed, pull the covers over her head and stay there.

Is this how her mother had felt?

Ivy turned out the lights and slowly made her way down the hallway. It was an effort to put one foot ahead of the other. In the bathroom she looked at herself in the mirror and wondered why her face still looked the same as it had that morning.

CHAPTER EIGHTEEN

Tomorrow I'll get what I need and set off into the bush. Everything's mega expensive here. So I'll take the bare minimum, I can live off the land.

From letters written by Roy Nolan,
April, 1972

THE NEXT MORNING, Tom landed the floatplane and taxied up to the dock at the lodge. Ivy hadn't spoken to him, and she looked as if she hadn't slept.

He sure as hell hadn't. Admitting what he'd done had left one big open wound. When he got home, Frances had already gone to her room and closed the door. He poured himself a scotch and bolted it down, but after two more stiff ones, he felt worse instead of better. It didn't stop him pouring another. So this morning he had a hangover.

"See you later," he called as Ivy bailed out of the plane. She lifted a hand without looking at him and hurried along the dock and up the path, taking the stairs two at a time as if she couldn't wait to get away from him.

He anchored the plane and followed her up, far more slowly. During the long and painful night, he'd gone over his life and decided he wasn't nearly done with being honest.

Ivy loved Ladrovik, and there, too, Tom had left a great deal unsaid. He should have told the younger man the truth about his conversation long ago with Roy Nolan. He could have given Alex a real feeling for what his father was like, and he hadn't, because that would've made him look bad.

Tom was going to do it now. He watched to make sure Ivy wasn't heading for Ladrovik's cabin, but she went around the back of the lodge, to the kitchen door.

Tom made his way to the cabin and banged on the door. He waited and, when there was no response, he opened it and stuck his head inside.

"Ladrovik?"

The bunk was stripped, cups were washed and in the drying rack beside the sink, the floor had been swept.

With a sense of foreboding, Tom turned toward the lodge.

"Morning, Tom." Oliver was heading for the tool shed.

Tom didn't bother with social niceties. "You happen to know where Ladrovik is?"

"Yeah, he packed up his gear and headed into town this morning on the boat—Grace had a doctor's appointment. They left maybe an hour ago."

Tom swallowed against the bile in his throat. "What sort of a pack did he take with him?"

"Just what he could carry—sleeping bag, rifle, survival stuff."

"Do you know exactly where he planned to head off into the bush?"

Oliver shrugged. "Dunno. He had some kind of map, but I didn't get a look at it. I think he left a copy with Theo, though."

"Thanks." With a growing sense of urgency, Tom headed for the lodge. Theo was sitting in the study, going over paperwork, a mug of coffee beside him. He smiled when Tom came in.

"Good to see you, Tom. Come and sit down."

Trying not to let the shock of Theo's frail appearance show in his expression, Tom shook his brother-in-law's hand and awkwardly clasped his shoulder hard, telling him how good it was to have him out of the hospital and back at the helm.

"Want some coffee?" Theo gestured at a carafe on his desk. "It's not the real stuff, they've got me on decaf. They changed my whole damned diet, even took my pipe away. I can't have half the stuff I love anymore."

"It's worth it if it keeps you healthy," Tom declared. The ache in his chest made him wonder if he wasn't about to follow in the other man's footsteps. He accepted the mug Theo handed him and sat in the armchair across from the desk, every muscle tense.

They talked for a few moments about family matters, but Tom had a hard time concentrating. Theo asked how Frances was, and Tom couldn't bring himself to mention the divorce. Not yet. He would, he vowed—he was through with keeping secrets—but at this moment, he was afraid he'd break down.

As soon as it was politely possible, Tom asked about Alex.

Theo confirmed that Alex had left that morning, early. "He came over and said goodbye last night. I made sure he was well equipped and that he had a good rifle. He's a fine young fellow, did a great job on those cabins while I was laid up. Wouldn't take anything for the extra work he did for me, either."

"Oliver said he might have left you a copy of the map he was planning to follow?"

"He did." Theo took it out of the desk drawer and handed it to Tom. "I told him about the public use cabins in the Chugach Forest. Long as he sticks to that map, there's several near his route. He ought to reach the first one in a couple, three days good walking."

"Mind if I have a copy of this?"

"Go right ahead. Use the fax over there, make yourself a copy."

As he did, Tom noticed that the public use cabins

were all located on water routes and accessible by floatplane.

Theo watched him study the map. His voice was diffident when he said, "Tom, I don't want to pry, but did Alex and Ivy have a falling out? I sure hope he played fair with her. I'd be very disappointed in him if he's let her down."

Tom had been too focused on his own conscience to even consider Ivy.

The weight of his responsibility grew even heavier. He knew Ivy was in love with Alex and he'd never interfered in his daughter's private affairs before. But he'd never felt as antagonistic toward any of the men she'd dated, either. Even before he knew who Ladrovik was, Tom had resented him.

He was beginning to understand why now. Frances was leaving him and he couldn't face losing Ivy as well, even to someone she loved. He was a selfish, self-serving bastard.

"I hope he treated her well, but I guess that's between them." Tom was in no position to judge. His need to find Ladrovik wasn't about Ivy, it was about his own guilty conscience—and the fact that he didn't want Alex to add to the number of people reported missing in the state of Alaska—3,300 last year alone. He didn't want him to disappear the way Roy Nolan had.

"So you're not going to track him down and beat

him senseless for walking out on her?" Theo made it sound like a joke, but there was more than a little concern underneath the banter.

"It's not about Ivy, Theo. It's about something I did a long time ago."

He could see the puzzlement on Theo's face. Much as it went against his reticent nature, Tom told him about that fateful morning he'd picked up a hitchhiker on the road to Anchorage.

"I didn't tell Alex the truth, and I should have."

Theo didn't make judgments, and Tom was grateful to him for it. "So now you're planning to track him down?"

"I'm going to try."

"Does Ivy know you're going after him?"

"Nope. I'd rather she didn't." Tom shook his head. This truth telling got complicated. One thing led straight to the next, and all of it was painful and humiliating. "She's got enough on her plate right at the moment." He forced the next words out. "Frances is leaving me. Ivy's all torn up about it."

"I'm sorry to hear that." Theo sounded sad but not surprised. Had he expected this? Tom wondered how much of life was ever the secret you believed it to be.

"She's been offered a job in New York, helping run a modeling agency, teaching older models. She's leaving in a couple weeks." Saying it hurt so much he almost doubled over from it. "She and Ivy have been at loggerheads for a long time—you probably know that. I couldn't let her blame Frances for this, so I told her about—" he cleared his throat "—about Mavis and me, what happened after my boy died." He stopped and drew a shaky breath. "I had to tell Ivy, she needs to know it was my fault."

"She'll get over it." Theo's voice was soothing. "It's always tough to find out your parents are only human. And don't go taking all the responsibility for the problems in your marriage, Tom. There's two of you involved."

Tom wasn't about to salve his conscience that way. "It was all me. I made a bad mistake. I've tried to make up for it over the years, but it's sat there like a boil, and now I guess it's reached a head and burst."

"Then maybe it'll heal. It was a long time ago."

The sound of the copter taking off reverberated through the room, and Tom got up and went to the window. He couldn't see the machine, but in his mind he flew it right along with Ivy.

"Weather's closing in, there's heavy rain in the long range forecast," Theo said from behind him. "Snow in the upper regions."

Tom nodded. Checking weather reports was second nature to a pilot.

"Ivy's a strong girl, Tom, she'll get through this."

"Yeah, she will." Tom had no doubt his girl would find a way to deal with it all, he knew the depths of her strength. But he also knew that nothing would ever be the same between them. He'd been a hero in Ivy's eyes, and that was over. He'd seen it in the look she gave him last night. He'd been a hero once with Frances, too. "Thanks for listening."

"Anytime. And if there's anything I can do, you let me know." Theo got up and took Tom's hand in both of his, holding on tighter and longer than usual. Tom's eyes smarted. His brother-in-law had become an old man in the past couple weeks.

They were both old men, come to that. "Thanks, Theo." His damned eyes were damp, and he had to swallow hard against the lump in his throat. Besides being a prize asshole, he was getting soft in his old age.

CHAPTER NINETEEN

There's all sorts of fantastic scenery in this town, but it's been raining a lot. I'm pretty much living on beans and bacon.

From letters written by Roy Nolan,
April, 1972

ALEX POUNDED IN the last tent stake and dropped to the ground, puffing. He was bone tired. He'd thought he was in top-notch condition, but he'd revised that misconception long before he pitched his tent late that first afternoon. There were varying degrees of physical fitness, and today had convinced him he was a long way from the top of the pyramid.

He'd chosen a high patch of ground surrounded by birch trees to make camp and, after a couple minutes, he got up and gathered rocks to make a fire pit. There was no shortage of water; a stream burbled along a few hundred feet below. It was still broad daylight. He figured he'd hiked maybe fifteen miles that first day.

The going had been tougher than he could ever have imagined. The ground was marshy. He'd had to cross several beaver ponds, and the icy water had sapped his energy. Now, the temperature was dropping as night approached.

He draped his wet pants over a makeshift rack near the fire, glad that he had warm, dry gear to change into and a well-insulated mummy bag. He also had survival rations, and he lit his small stove and dropped one of the freeze-dried envelopes into a Billy can of water along with a handful of rice. It didn't compare to Mavis's meals, but that didn't stop him from wolfing it down.

His father wouldn't have had anything like this to eat. Roy would have had to fish or hunt, which took up a great deal of time. From the little Tom had said, Roy probably didn't have a decent rifle, either, and certainly not a compact tent like Alex's.

Many of the supplies Alex had bought at a climber's specialty store in San Diego hadn't been readily available in the early '70s, even if Nolan had had the money to buy them. Which he hadn't, Alex knew from Roy's journal. He'd made this trip on a shoestring.

The fire was soothing, and he propped his back against a log, soaking in the heat. It reminded him of evenings in the cabin with Ivy, heater going full blast, the two of them naked underneath the duvet. The memory brought regret, and loneliness.

She'd been in the back of his mind all day. Once, he'd heard a plane, and his heart swelled at the thought that it might be her. The sky was overcast, and he hadn't been able to locate the plane. When the sound dwindled, he'd felt ridiculously abandoned.

That plane was the only sign of human contact he'd had all day, and he was beginning to sympathize a little more with Ivy's strong feelings about people who headed off into the bush. They didn't know what they were getting into, she insisted, and he had to admit she was right. He'd thought he was prepared, but one day had shown him he wasn't.

The terrain he'd crossed that day was unbelievably rugged. He'd heard Oliver say that someone unfamiliar with Alaska could go a mile, two miles, from the lodge and never be seen again. Alex had thought that was a gross exaggeration. Now, he knew it was absolutely true.

He'd also heard Ben and the guides discussing end-of-the-roaders—the local name for people running from something, or seeking one last chance, dreamers and schemers and loners, and those with a death wish.

"If someone wants to drop off the face of the earth and never be heard from again, Alaska's the place to do it," Ben had concluded. "People simply vanish up here. Water accidents and drowning probably account for more than half of the thousands who go missing each year. In water as cold as this, bodies that sink stay sunk. They don't decompose and float to the surface."

Alex shuddered. So had Roy Nolan been an end-of-the-roader with a death wish? His letters didn't indicate that, but Alex didn't know enough about the stranger who was his biological father to know for sure. As for himself, it had only taken him a few hours this first day to figure out the answer.

He was neither. No end-of-the-roader, not a guy with a death wish. A fool, certainly, because he hadn't known until he left how much he cared for Ivy. With every step he took away from her, the desire to go back to her intensified.

Several times during this long and difficult day, in fact, he'd seriously considered turning around. But he'd made a commitment, albeit to himself, and he was going to stick to it. Otherwise, it could someday come back to haunt him. But once the trip was over, once he'd followed as much of Nolan's map as he could, he'd head back to Valdez. Back to Ivy. He had no idea yet what he'd say to her, but he had plenty of time to figure that out. First thing he'd do was apologize, that was a given.

He took the worn photo of Annie out of his pocket. Did Roy carry a photo of Linda? Or his newborn son? The letters didn't say.

"Your old man's not the brightest, kid." His jaws

ached from yawning. He tucked the snap back inside the zippered pocket on his windbreaker and banked the fire. He'd made it safely through the first day of his pilgrimage, and there was satisfaction in that.

As he zipped the sleeping bag around him he wondered if Roy had been as fortunate. Had he managed to stay alive even one day?

But Alex's last thought before sleep claimed him wasn't of Nolan or Linda—or even of Annie. It was Ivy. He wished he'd waited for her this morning. He ought to have told her goodbye.

HE HADN'T EVEN WAITED to say goodbye to her.

Ivy flew her clients as close as she dared to the bald eagles' nests hidden in crags on the rocky mountain slopes. But her mind kept straying to the scene in the kitchen at the lodge earlier than morning.

Mavis was the one who'd told her Alex was gone.

"He came in to say goodbye before I even had the coffee made. I packed him up a lunch, some of these raisin scones you both like so much and a couple good thick ham sandwiches. Maybe I should have put rat poison in instead of butter?" she'd added with a questioning look at Ivy.

"Yeah." Before, Ivy might have told Mavis everything, but her feelings toward the woman had changed. It was a challenge now, to treat Mavis the same as always.

It was also a challenge to do her usual guest lecture.

"The eagles migrate once a year," she recited to her customers, angling the copter so they could get a good look at another nest. "As many as 3500 gather along the Chilkat River north of Haines, usually in late October. They come to feed on the chum salmon run. It's a spectacle that now attracts almost as many tourists as there are birds."

The more she thought about it, the more Ivy suspected her aunt and uncle, her cousins—maybe the whole town of Valdez for all she knew—were privy to secrets that had been kept from her. She was outraged.

Keep your mind on the job, Ivy. "Bald eagles are on the endangered species list everywhere else, but here in Alaska, they're thriving."

She'd had a right to know, too, hadn't she? She wasn't a child, needing protection. And with that sense of outrage came a strange new loyalty toward Frances. Her mother had been a victim, and that brought out a protectiveness Ivy hadn't felt before.

She realized suddenly that she was getting dangerously close to a snow-capped mountain peak, and she lifted the copter up and over in a stomach-dropping maneuver. The tiny woman sitting beside her gripped the handhold above her head and gave an involuntary shriek, her eyes filled with terror.

"Sorry about that." *Damn.* She'd lost concentration, and that was inexcusable. Hadn't Tom always told her that a pilot had to leave personal problems on the ground?

She was going to take a couple days off, Ivy decided. It had always been easy for her to leave her problems on the ground, but it wasn't working this time. This time she needed to get her head together before she could safely fly again.

There was a storm coming. The ominous dark clouds were still off in the distance, but it was time to head back to Valdez.

TOM WAS FINISHING what he called the weekly milk runs, dropping off groceries, liquor and supplies to three isolated fishing camps along the Katalla River. In the past two hours, the weather had deteriorated, just as the weatherman had predicted. The sky was now heavily overcast and rain pelted on the Beaver's windshield as he lifted off the water and banked in a slow turn. He'd told Kisha he'd stay in camp if the storm socked in, but he figured there was enough of a window to get back to Valdez.

The nagging concern over Ladrovik had grown more acute than ever the past two days, and impulsively he turned up the river, following it toward the general location of the first public cabin.

He'd just do a quick reconnaissance and see if there was any sign of Ladrovik yet. It was probably too soon. Wouldn't hurt to look, though. Maybe he'd land, do some fishing, wait out the storm there. Kill two birds with one stone.

After ten minutes of flying, fog began rolling in along with the rain. He ought to turn back and try again when the weather cleared. But according to reports, the storm was going to last several days. Flying would be dicey, maybe impossible.

Would Ladrovik do the sensible thing and hole up in the cabin? Tom had no idea. He only knew that one more sleepless night was more than he could face.

Ivy hadn't been in touch, and when he called her house all he got was the answering machine, even though he suspected she was home. He needed to make things right with Alex before he could begin to mend his relationship with his daughter.

The fog was growing thicker. Dropping low, he spotted the lake and cabin.

Steering the plane downward, he made the usual visual check before he set down on the water.

He was throttling back when the skid hit the deadhead. The impact was violent. Before he could even take a breath, the plane was upside down, and Tom's head smashed hard against the roof.

When he came to seconds later, instinct made him want to pull back on the control column in a vain effort to get the plane up and out of the water, but years of experience stopped him. He knew the emergency procedure, but executing it was something else again.

Everything was black, he was upside down and water was pouring in. He could feel himself panicking, but he fought it with every fiber of his being. The only way he was going to survive was to stay strapped in his seat belt until the aircraft stopped moving and settled deep in the water. He had to let the pressure inside and out equalize so he'd be able to open the door. And pray there'd be some small pocket of air trapped inside for him to breathe. The icy water was rising fast, already past his chest, numbing him. He drew in a lungful of air, and then another. The water reached his neck.

The plane was settling slowly, way too slowly. He knew there was a life jacket under the other seat and, if he was to survive, he had to find it. He took a breath and ducked under the water, searching.

It seemed forever before his fingers closed over it. Gripping it hard in his right hand, he slid it over his forearm and undid his seat belt while grappling with the door handle.

It took all his strength to finally force it open, shove himself through it and then kick for the surface. The water was liquid ice.

He could feel himself weakening.

CHAPTER TWENTY

I dreamed of you last night, you were wearing that blue dress. Hang on to that dress, okay, Lindy?

From letters written by Roy Nolan,
April, 1972

IT WAS THE LIFE JACKET that saved Tom, pulling him up toward light and air without much help from him. His head broke the surface and he gasped for breath, his body nearly paralyzed by the cold. He choked and gagged before finally getting air into his lungs. The cold was sapping his remaining strength, and he began struggling to the shoreline, toward the cabin that was now nearly invisible in the rain.

It seemed an eternity passed before his hands and knees finally hit gravel. Dazed and exhausted, he crawled out of the water and slumped on the muddy earth, soaking wet, panting and shuddering with cold.

At last he mustered enough energy to get to his feet and stagger in the direction of the cabin. He was dizzy and nearly frozen. He felt nauseated, his crippled leg was next to useless, and he fell heavily every few steps. Each time he considered not getting up again. The thick undergrowth dragged at his heavy, wet boots and tree branches slapped at his face.

He forced himself to move, and at last he staggered, one dragging step after the other, to the cabin. He stopped short.

The cabin door was wide open. Toilet paper, spilled coffee, flour, packets of dried soup and a broken, empty jar of molasses littered the area. An animal had broken in, probably a grizzly by the size of the deep gouges on the door.

Tom stood still, listening for any sound that might indicate the bear was still around. If it was, his life was over. He had no weapon and he couldn't run. He sniffed, trying to detect the distinctive musk. After a few moments, he dared a few lurching steps forward.

The cabin was empty. It had been ransacked, but there was no bear in sight. He muttered a prayer of thanks and dragged the heavy door shut behind him. But that made the interior so dark, he couldn't see anything, so he shoved it open again. If the bear was coming back, it would make short work of the door anyway.

He had to get a fire going, but he was so dizzy he slumped for a moment into a chair that had somehow stayed upright.

Tom was a longtime resident of Alaska, and he knew exactly how precarious his situation was. All his emergency supplies, including the rifle he carried in the floatplane, were at the bottom of the lake. Without a gun, he had no protection if the grizzly returned. He probably had a concussion from the blow on his head. He reached up and touched it, and his fingers came away bloody.

No one would be looking for him soon. The office was empty. Kisha had gone to Anchorage that afternoon with Bert. Because he and Ivy weren't communicating the way they normally did, she wouldn't be suspicious. She'd probably stay at the lodge tonight, so she wouldn't notice the floatplane was missing.

Tom's spirits dropped even lower. He wanted to stagger to the bunk and just lie there until oblivion rescued him. But he fought the impulse.

He had to dry off. That meant getting a fire going in the barrel stove in the corner, which miraculously was still intact. There were logs and kindling in a box near the heater. Tom just had to find matches. He staggered over to the cupboards, but the bear had pretty much cleaned everything out, knocking the contents to the floor in its search for food.

Tom lowered himself to his hands and knees and, shivering hard, started scrabbling through the debris on the floor. The matches ought to be in a waterproof container, but he couldn't find them in the mess. He was so cold he could barely move. There was a blanket on the bunk, and he wrapped it around himself, again struggling against the urge to just lie down and let himself drift off. The dizziness was getting worse, and his stomach roiled each time he bent over.

He fought against the nausea, cursing and praying as he dug through the mess the bear had made, and at last by some miracle he found the matches. They were in a small aluminum cylinder that had rolled under the bunk. He belly crawled under it to retrieve them, and then could barely wriggle his way out again.

He pulled himself to his feet and staggered over to the stove where he crumpled paper and added kindling. It caught right away and soon the fire was crackling. Closing the cabin door, he started peeling off his sodden clothing, wringing each garment out as best he could, and draped them over the chairs he'd dragged close to the heater.

Wrapped only in the wool blanket, he scavenged for food. He felt nauseous, but he knew he needed the energy.

A public cabin usually had emergency rations, but the bear had demolished most of them. Tom found a tin of beans in a corner and the opener in a drawer. He set the opened tin on the stove to warm, but he was too exhausted to wait. He found a spoon and shoveled as many mouthfuls down as he could tolerate. He stoked the heater and then, wrapped in the blanket, he half fell onto the bunk and slipped into oblivion.

When he woke again his stomach was cramping, and he vomited up the beans, barely able to hold his head over the edge of the bunk. He was shuddering with cold even though he was burning with fever. His head felt as if it was about to explode. He had no idea where he was. Dim light sifted through the windows.

Mustn't let the fire go out—

It took a long time before he could force himself out of the bunk to add logs to the embers. He stayed by the stove for a long time, curled on the wooden floor, slipping in and out of delirium. He saw the bear come back, heard Frances say she was leaving him to go live with Mavis, dreamed he was back in Vietnam. He looked up and saw Ivy at the controls of a helicopter that was out of control, spiraling down from the sky at deadly speed, and he screamed and wept.

In the few moments he was lucid, he added wood to the stove, but his supply was dwindling fast. He knew he didn't have strength enough to go outside and find more, and Tom accepted that this was the way he was going to die.

He wasn't afraid of death. He'd seen far too much of it in Vietnam to have any fear left. There was nothing more he could do for Frances, or for Ivy, either. But he felt great sadness and remorse and, for the first time in years, he prayed, asking that he be spared long enough to make things right with Alex.

CHAPTER TWENTY-ONE

I wish there was somebody besides that dipstick friend of yours who'd keep an eye out for you and the sprout until I get back from this odyssey.

From letters written by Roy Nolan,
April, 1972

IVY WAITED a full day, trying to build up her nerve, before she called her mother. Her throat was dry as she dialed. She hadn't spoken to Frances since that terrible scene in the office. She'd spent hours wondering what to say and how to say it, and all she knew for sure was that the telephone wasn't the way to do it.

So when Frances answered, Ivy blurted out, "I wondered if you'd like to come over and have supper with me tonight, Mom? I'm making—" Damn, she hadn't thought that far ahead yet. "Actually I'm not sure what I'm making yet." And then she remembered that Frances taught night school. She ought to know which nights, but she didn't. She didn't really know much about her mother's life at all.

"But if you're teaching, we could do it another time."

Except that she wanted to get this over with now.

She could hear the surprise in Frances's voice. "I'm not teaching, and I'd love to come. What time, Ivy?"

"Early. Five?"

"Five is great." When Ivy didn't say anything else, Frances added, "See you later, then."

That afternoon, Ivy was finishing last-minute preparations when Frances knocked. It was indicative of their relationship that her mother would wait for Ivy to come answer the door. Tom never did.

"Hi, dear." Frances took off her suede jacket and hung it on one of the pegs just inside the door, then tugged off her boots and slipped on a pair of scarlet embroidered Chinese slippers she'd brought with her. She was wearing jeans with a simple white cashmere sweater and her trademark silver jewelry. Her hair was swept up in a messy knot. She looked beautiful, and for a moment Ivy felt as she always had around her mother—insecure, off balance, unattractive. She was going to change that, she vowed. It had nothing to do with Frances, and everything to do with her own self-worth.

"It smells wonderful in here." Frances was obviously not going to mention the way they'd parted at the office the other day. "What are you making?"

"Seafood quiche." Ivy led the way into the

kitchen, where she'd covered the small wooden table with a daisy-print cloth and laid out her plain white dishes. She'd never before had Frances for a meal just on her own, and Ivy had grown more nervous as the day progressed.

"Sit down, Mom. Would you like some wine?"

"Please."

Ivy opened the bottle and poured two goblets. She raised hers in a salute. "Here's to your new life, Mom. I hope you'll be happy. I know you'll be successful."

"Oh, Ivy. Oh, thank you so much." Frances's eyes welled with tears. "That means everything, coming from you."

Ivy swallowed a big gulp of wine for courage and plowed on. "I'm sorry about the other day—I said things I shouldn't have."

Frances was obviously having as much difficulty with this as Ivy was. She brushed away tears with the back on her hand. "It was a shock for you. I'm really sorry I didn't tell you sooner, Ivy."

"You tried. I just didn't stick around long enough to listen." Ivy rubbed her damp palms down her pants and grabbed oven mitts to take the quiche out of the oven. She set it on the table, then got the salad out of the fridge.

"I hope this is done." Ivy carefully put a generous slice on each of their plates, along with salad.

"Mmm. This is fabulous."

"Thanks, I got the recipe from—" From Mavis. Ivy couldn't hold back any longer. She laid down her fork.

"Dad told me, Mom."

"Told you what?" Frances was suddenly wary.

"About...about him and...and Mavis." Ivy gulped. "About the affair. After Jacob died?"

"Oh. That." Frances sighed and sipped her wine. "Old news, my dear. And he shouldn't have said anything, after all this time."

"Yes, he should." Ivy's tone was vehement. "I didn't know. All these years, I thought...I believed...I didn't..." She drew a sobbing breath. "I blamed you for everything, Mom. Why didn't you tell me? Why didn't you ever say? I'm almost thirty, I should have known long ago. Because I've gone this whole time thinking—believing—that you, that he—"

"Oh, sweetheart." Frances shook her head, her eyes sad. "I couldn't tell you. How could I do such a mean, petty thing? Tom practically raised you on his own—he had to. The two of you are so close."

Ivy nodded. "I always felt responsible for your depression, Mom. I always thought that if I was prettier or if I liked clothes or if I didn't get grease on me or something—"

Frances was openly sobbing now. She dabbed at her eyes with her napkin, and then got up to get a handful of tissues from her handbag. She blew her nose and made an obvious effort to control herself.

On her way back to her seat, she tentatively touched Ivy's shoulder.

"Oh, dearest, you had nothing to do with it. I'm so *sorry* you ever felt that way." Frances suddenly wrapped her arms around Ivy's shoulders, startling both of them. "You're perfect just as you are, you must know that."

Ivy had no idea that's what her mother thought. As quickly as she'd hugged her, Frances pulled away. She sat back down, across from Ivy.

"How could I know. This is the first time you've ever said anything like that to me." Her voice wavered on the words. She was having such a hard time with this. She was exposing her most wounded places to the one person she'd never trusted.

"I'm so incredibly sorry, Ivy." Frances took a deep breath and let it out again. "I've always had such a hard time talking about the things that really matter. And I've gone for years blaming Tom for what were really my problems."

"But how could he *do* such a thing, Mom?" It was almost a wail. "How could he have an affair with *Mavis?* Especially just when you must have really needed him?"

"Losing a child does strange things to people," Frances said in a quiet tone. "There's no predicting how it will affect you."

Alex had said almost the exact same thing.

"But...you must hate her, Mom. You must feel so betrayed. I could hardly speak to her the other morning. I really see now why you hardly ever visit the lodge. And *why* would Aunt Caitlin ask her to live with them, when she must have known how you felt about Mavis? *She* betrayed you as well."

"That happened years later, Ivy. You must have been about ten when Caitlin brought Mavis back to the lodge. You see, Mavis left Alaska after I found out about the affair. I made a really terrible scene."

"I guess you had good reason."

Frances smiled a little. "I thought so at the time. I was very angry, and I wasn't about to take responsibility for anything in those days. Anyway, Mavis left for Seattle and got married. That's where the pressure cooker blew up and she was burned."

Ivy shuddered. The extent of Mavis's injuries... they were horrifying.

"Physically, Mavis healed. But mentally, she deteriorated," Frances explained. "Her husband disappeared, she couldn't take care of herself—she was placed in an institution."

"I didn't know that." Ivy lifted her glass to her mouth, but she found she couldn't swallow.

"Before she brought Mavis back here, Cait asked me how I'd feel about it. Well, Mavis had no other relatives who were willing to take her in. I'm afraid I was anything but gracious." Frances's smile was sad.

"Cait brought her anyway." Ivy was having trouble letting go of the smoldering anger she'd felt ever since Tom had told her his part of the story. "You'd think Aunt Cait would have respected how you felt, Mom. After all, you were family."

"So was Mavis. Your father felt deeply responsible for what had happened to her, of course. Cait signed her out of the awful place she was in and brought her back to the lodge. It was hard at first, Mavis cried continually and wouldn't see anyone. But gradually, she got better. She started cooking again, and that helped. But she's never been able to be around me. She gets hysterical. That's why I seldom go there, and when I do, Cait makes sure Mavis isn't around."

Ivy's head was swimming. There were so many layers to this, so much she'd never understood. So much she'd assumed without knowing the real truth.

"In those days, I didn't understand at all about depression, Ivy. Not many people did. It wasn't until you were a teenager that I finally got the courage to see a psychiatrist. You remember the trip we took to New York for your sixteenth birthday?"

"Yeah." Ivy made a face. "Man, I hated New York. And I made sure you knew it."

Frances laughed. "You were pretty awful, all right, but the trip was good for me. The psychiatrist diagnosed depression and gave me medication. It helped, although it didn't get to the root of the problem. It was Libby Santana who helped me confront the things I'd been running away from most of my life."

"Libby? But I thought Libby was a nurse." Ivy'd never really gotten to know Frances's friend. She hadn't bothered to get to know any of her mother's friends.

"She is a nurse, she's a psych nurse. She's also a really wise woman."

"I don't understand what you've been running from." Ivy regretted the words before they were even out of her mouth. She ought to know better than to push her mother about the past. Frances would close down, cut her off, make her feel stupid. Ivy got to her feet, reached for Frances's plate. "I guess I should clear this away, it's cold by now anyway."

But Frances stopped her. "Don't, please. I want to tell you everything. But if you can wait to hear it, let's eat this wonderful meal you've prepared first. We can microwave our plates, can't we?"

"I'll stick them in." At least Frances had found a gentler way of avoiding what she didn't want to talk about.

They ate, chatting about the job Frances was going to in New York and the tourists Ivy had taken on the eagle tour, both of them carefully avoiding mention of Tom. When they were done, Frances helped clear the table and insisted on washing up the few dishes. Afterwards, she dried her hands and rubbed lotion into them.

"Is there coffee? And maybe we could finish up that great wine," she added with a rueful smile. "Truth is, I might need more than a little liquor to get through what I have to say."

Wondering what was coming, Ivy brought a tray to the living room and poured coffee for them both, automatically adding the rich cream and sugar both she and her mother liked. She refilled their wine-glasses and sat across from Frances.

Her mother was visibly nervous. She twisted her rings, fiddled with her heavy silver bracelet.

"You know I came from a small town in Ohio."

Ivy nodded. "Yes, Brigham Falls." And that was all she knew. Her anticipation was growing, and her dread. What was so horrible that her mother couldn't speak of it?

"I was born into a religious community that believed in polygamy," Frances said. Her voice was trembling. "I was the twenty-sixth child of Leander Mathews, born to his fifth wife, Evelyn. My mother was sixteen when she had me—I was her second baby. My sister, also Evelyn, was only ten months older than me. The last time I saw any of them, I was fourteen years old."

CHAPTER TWENTY-TWO

I think about you a lot and I get homesick sometimes. I hope the money I left lasts until I get back.

From letters written by Roy Nolan,
April, 1972

IVY WAS DUMBFOUNDED. "Oh, Mom. Oh, my God." She'd imagined so many things over the years, but she could never have come close to this incredible truth.

"God, indeed." Frances's smile was enigmatic. "They believed they were following His instructions, as in, go forth and multiply. They weren't evil, Ivy. They were just so convinced their way was the only way." Frances lifted her coffee cup to her lips, holding it with both hands to keep from spilling.

"When I was fourteen," she went on, "my father married me to a fifty-six-year-old who had seven other wives." She shuddered. "I loathed the man, and I begged my mother, but she had no say in the matter. So I did the only thing I could do. I ran away."

"Oh, Mom." Ivy took her mother's hand. The feel of her soft, smooth skin moved Ivy to tears. "Mom, I'm *so sorry.*"

Fourteen. She'd have been unprepared and terrified at fourteen. That was when she'd been learning to fly—her father teaching her everything he knew about safety.

Frances gripped Ivy's hand tighter. Her eyes were infinitely sad. "While I was hitchhiking, making my escape, I was raped by a truck driver. He felt guilty and gave me some money, which is how I finally made it to New York."

Ivy could feel the fine tremors in her mother's hand.

"I got a job washing dishes at a greasy spoon," France said. "One day on the 57th Street crosstown bus, the wife of a staff photographer for *Vogue* saw me and asked if I'd pose for her husband. At first I thought it was a trap of some kind, I'd gotten pretty streetwise by then. But she convinced me. And it turned out I had some instinctive connection to the camera, and they gave me a lot of help. Gertrude and Sam Balkin. They took me into their home and treated me so well. Two years later I was on the cover of *Vogue.*"

"You were just a kid." The story broke Ivy's heart.

"I grew up fast. I was almost sixteen by then, that's actually mature for a fashion model by today's standards."

"But being famous—it must have been such a change for you."

"It was. We didn't earn the huge money that today's megamodels earn, but it was still more money than I'd ever dreamed of." Frances shook her head, her eyes haunted. "And oh, Ivy, it did me so much harm."

Ivy waited silently. This was like hearing about a stranger. Frances *was* a stranger, she realized with a sense of wonder. This woman had given birth to her, but Ivy knew so little about her.

"As I became more and more popular and in demand, I started to think I was really somebody. I wouldn't take any advice from Sam or Gertrude, and after a quarrel about a man I was dating, I moved out of their house and into his apartment. I was running with a fast crowd. I did drugs. I got hooked." She wasn't looking at Ivy now. Her head was bowed, her hands fisted into knots. Ivy had to strain to hear her.

"I got pregnant. I had abortions." At the agony in her mother's voice, Ivy reached across and squeezed her arm. "Three, before I was twenty. The last one caused a serious infection. The doctors said I'd be lucky to ever have a full-term pregnancy."

Frances was watching her face now, watching her reactions, and hard as she tried she couldn't hide her shock and horror.

"I couldn't have more children after you were born. It was a miracle I had the two of you."

Ivy couldn't think of anything to say. Her heart

actually hurt for her mother, and she pressed a hand to her chest.

"You see why I couldn't ever bring myself to tell you all this, Ivy?" Frances asked. "I couldn't bear to talk about it, I was so ashamed. So dreadfully ashamed. I thought you'd hate me if you ever found out."

Would she have, Ivy wondered? Or would it have made her feel what she was feeling right now: overwhelming compassion and pity…and love. So much love it was painful.

"Anyhow, of course I crashed," Frances said. "What with the drugs and the abortions, and the man I thought I loved seducing girls I thought were my friends right in front of me. I was so desperately unhappy I tried suicide. I swallowed pills. One of the other models found me, took me to hospital. That was just before I had to come to Alaska for the photo shoot."

"When you met Dad," Ivy whispered.

"I was very fragile, and Tom was so strong, Ivy. So reliable, so different in every way from the men I knew in New York. He saved my life. He helped me kick the drugs. He'd seen so much of it in Vietnam he knew exactly what to do."

"Did—did you love him?" It seemed so important to know that.

Frances didn't hesitate. "Of *course* I loved him. I still do, Ivy. Tom is the only man I've ever loved. The only man I could ever love."

The declaration eased some deep pain in Ivy. "In spite of the affair?"

"I didn't think so for a long while, but now..." Frances slowly nodded. "I understand now how frightened and alone he must have felt. I was so immature, such a child, Ivy. I had nothing to offer, I was just not there for anyone, least of all myself or him. He'd just lost his son, he had you to take care of, he was overwhelmed... I see that so clearly now."

"Then—then why can't you stay with him? Why can't you work things out with Dad?" Ivy didn't feel like an adult at this moment. She felt like a little girl who wanted nothing more than her mother and father, together.

"I can't, dear." Frances thought for a moment. "Leaving isn't about not loving him, or not loving you," she said. "It's about me. I need to see if I've got what it takes to grow up, finally."

"Couldn't you stay and do that here?"

"Oh, Ivy." There was despair in Frances's voice. "I've been trying to, for about five years now. Ever since I started teaching, ever since I started working with Libby. I've tried to get Tom to go to counseling with me, but he won't."

This Ivy understood. She knew her father, knew exactly how he'd react to that suggestion.

"Libby warned me that when one partner in a marriage begins to change, it's very hard on the other person," Frances explained. "Unless they change as well, the relationship can't survive."

Ivy slowly nodded. "Not just in a marriage. In any relationship." She looked at her mother, woman to woman. "Dad really isn't into change. Or talking to a stranger, either. He even hates that word, *relationship.*"

"I know. But even if he agreed to counseling, I'd still have to leave, Ivy."

"Yeah." Her sigh felt as if it came from her toes. "I see that." It sounded so familiar. "Alex said exactly the same thing before he dumped me." And with that, Ivy couldn't hold it together any longer. She burst into tears, sobbing uncontrollably.

Her mother had never been demonstrative. Ivy smelled L'Air du Temps, her mother's perfume and felt Frances's arms encircle her tentatively, then tighten.

Frances didn't say anything. She patted Ivy's back and murmured wordless loving sounds that slowly penetrated the misery and eased the pain in her daughter's heart.

Finally Ivy pulled away. She went into the bathroom and composed herself, blotting at her eyes as she came out.

Frances was waiting in the living room, still sitting on the sofa. She patted the cushion next to her and Ivy sank down, pulling her legs up under her.

Frances had poured fresh coffee. She handed a

mug to Ivy and said, "Tell me exactly what happened with Alex, please."

Ivy went through it all. She knew it off by heart, word for word. "And he said when he got back to Valdez he had to pick up his Jeep anyway, so he'd probably see me. Maybe even for two days before he took off again, lucky me." As miserable as recounting it made her feel, Ivy couldn't miss the stricken look on her mother's face.

"And this happened when?"

"Two nights ago. No, three."

"I met him that very afternoon." Frances sounded guilty.

"He told me." Ivy felt hot color stain her cheeks when she remembered the unkind things she'd said about Frances.

"Ivy, I think I made a terrible mistake that day." Frances got to her feet and walked to the window. With her back turned, she said, "I think it was my fault that Alex left the way he did, said the things he did."

Frances turned from the window, faced Ivy. "You see, I—I told Alex you were in love with him."

Ivy thought that her capacity for surprise was on overload, but she was wrong. For a moment, she just stared at her mother in disbelief. Then she sprang to her feet, pacing as she digested this latest piece of news.

"*Why?* Why did you do that, Mom? How did you even know?"

"Tom told me." The three words were quiet. "You're what we talk about now, Ivy. You're what we have left, the best part of our marriage. I asked what was going on with you, and Tom told me you were in love."

"I didn't tell him, because I guess I knew it would drive him away. He told me in the beginning not to pin any hopes on the long term."

Frances's face showed the anguish she was feeling. "I'm so awfully sorry, Ivy. I thought it was reciprocal between the two of you, and I wanted Alex to know that I—I cared about you, that I was concerned for your happiness."

Ivy could hear the sincerity in her mother's tone, but it didn't ease the hurt.

"I also sensed that Tom had some issues with Alex, and I guess in some selfish way, after I'd met him I wanted Alex to know that your parents weren't united on that score. That I'd come to my own conclusions about him." She got up and stood in front of Ivy. Her eyes were sad. "Do you want me to leave?"

"No. Stay." Ivy was surprised at her immediate response. "But I need to move. Let's go outside, okay? Let's go for a walk."

They put on jackets and boots and headed down the quiet street, their long strides unconsciously in synch. They didn't talk much. Several neighbors passed them and made comments on the weather—chilly today and windy. More rain forecast. Frances responded with appropriate comments so Ivy didn't have to.

Walking didn't change anything, but it made her feel less desperate. They'd been gone about a half hour when she said, "Maybe it was the best thing, Mom. It would have happened eventually anyway, and it would have hurt just as much. So don't feel guilty about it, okay? I'll get over it." She managed a wry laugh. "Part of it's just my pride—I've always been the one to do the dumping. It's really hell to be on the receiving end."

"Isn't it?"

"*You* got dumped?" She turned and stared at her mother.

"Big time." And for the next ten minutes, as they made their way down to the wharf, Frances told her such a humorous story, Ivy couldn't help laughing.

She hadn't forgotten about Alex, but at least she could laugh again.

CHAPTER TWENTY-THREE

The weather's still no hell, rainy and cold, but with May almost here it'll soon get warmer. At least there's no bugs, so it balances out.

From letters written by Roy Nolan,
April, 1972

ALEX WAS WET to the skin and fed up to the teeth. He'd just forded a swift-flowing, icy-cold river, and he'd lost his footing.

Weighted down by his pack and unable to get enough leverage to stand up again, he'd had a few desperate moments when he thought he was going to drown. And in those moments he fully appreciated what could have happened to Roy Nolan. There were innumerable ways to die in this unforgiving country.

"You're a damned fool," he told himself after he'd struggled out of the water and stripped off his dripping jeans and shirt. Shoulders hunched against the icy wind, he tugged on dry clothes, shivering so hard he could barely do the buttons up on his shirt.

Thank God he'd had enough foresight to roll his extra pants and shirt and socks in plastic, so they were relatively dry. His gun, too, was wrapped in oilskin and then plastic. The survival manuals he'd studied had recommended that.

He made the change as fast as possible, not only because he was freezing in the cold wind, but also because he felt really vulnerable being bare-assed naked in a place where bears could appear without much warning.

It was one thing to confront a grizzly while you were fully clothed, gun in hand. Quite another with your balls bare. He'd seen one not twenty feet away earlier that day, and it was hours before his heart had stopped hammering.

Chewing on a protein bar, he studied the map Theo had given him that showed the location of the public cabins. He must be only a few miles from the first one, and the thought of sleeping under a roof was powerfully appealing.

The going was rough. In spots the faint trail threatened to disappear completely, and the cold wind had picked up again. To take his mind off his physical discomfort, Alex thought about Ivy. He'd thought about little else the past two days.

The farther away from her he traveled, the more his feelings intensified. At some point he'd admitted to himself that he loved her. He'd fought it, but it happened in spite of his intentions, and now it felt right. If he got out of this alive, he wanted to spend whatever life he had left with her.

Alex knew from the letters that Roy came to feel the same way about his mother as he struggled along this godforsaken trail. Roy realized at the end that the deeper meaning he was searching for in his life really lay with the woman and baby he'd left behind.

As Alex climbed over deadfalls and waded through yet another beaver pond, other things he'd either buried or avoided came to the surface. Today he found he was thinking a lot about his relationship—or lack of relationship—with Steve Ladrovik.

Ivy had pointed out that at least Steve was there when Alex was growing up. Roy wasn't. That had irritated and angered Alex at the time, because his childhood would have been a lot less traumatic without Ladrovik beating on him regularly. Steve's temper and moods had dominated Alex's early life.

When Steve died, Alex hadn't felt sadness or remorse. He still didn't, but in spite of everything, he owed the man a debt of gratitude. Steve had adopted him, insisted on raising him as his own son. He'd paid for that first critical year of his university education. It was little enough, but he'd done it. There must have been many times when Steve wanted to tell Alex they weren't really related, that no son of his would do or act or be the way Alex was.

But he hadn't. He'd kept it to himself, maintained the facade that Alex was his biological son. Why? Alex pondered it as he forced his tired legs up a steep incline.

Where the hell was that cabin? He felt as if he'd been walking for half his life. But then the wind shifted and he smelled wood smoke. So he must be close, but someone else was in residence.

Alex hesitated. Maybe they wouldn't welcome a visitor.

The sky had gradually been growing darker, and now it began to rain. The wind drove the icy drops straight at him, and he could hardly see. He decided that whether or not he was welcome, he was going to the cabin anyway.

He checked his compass and quickened his steps. By the time he stumbled down a slippery hill and broke through the trees to the rocky shore of a small lake, he'd had more than enough hiking for the day.

The lake the cabin was on was small by Alaskan standards. Alex used the compass again, following the shoreline until he finally came to the clearing with the cabin.

He stopped and stared at the devastation around the door, realizing that a bear must have ransacked the place. But the trickle of smoke coming from the chimney meant that whoever was inside was human.

The door was shut. Alex knocked and knocked again, louder. "Hello, in there!" he hollered. "Can I come in and get dry?"

He tried the latch, but it was fastened from inside. They didn't want visitors, that was pretty clear.

"Hello!" he bellowed again. "I won't stay long, I just want to dry some of my clothes, I fell in the river."

He heard a loud thump, like someone falling. There was silence, and then the sound of something heavy being dragged across the floor.

Alex steeled himself. He wondered if he ought to leave, fast. He took a couple of steps back.

From inside there was muffled cursing, a fumbling at the latch. The door opened inward, and after a stunned moment, Alex grabbed for Tom's arm and steadied him, just in time to keep him from slipping to the floor. He was naked except for a gray blanket clutched around his shoulders.

Tom was shivering, although his face was flushed and perspiring. A deep gash above his forehead extended up past his hairline, and his hair was matted with dried blood.

"Ladrovik," Tom said in a weak, congested echo of his usual deep growl. "What the hell took you so long?"

He wobbled, and Alex dumped his backpack and then slid an arm around Tom's torso and half carried him over to the bunk, which held only a bare mattress. He eased Tom down and wrapped the blanket around him.

The cabin was dark and chilly, the fire barely going. There was a pool of vomit on the floor beside the bunk, and only one small log left beside the stove. The flannel shirt and denim pants draped around it were sodden.

Alex shoved the log into the flames and turned back to Tom. "I'm going outside to get wood, warm it up in here."

He wondered if Tom even heard him, but then he coughed and grunted. "I'm not going anywhere."

"Glad to hear it." Alex unpacked his sleeping bag and tucked it around the shivering man. Then he took the small ax from the side of his pack and headed outside.

The bear hadn't disturbed the neat stack of firewood along one side of the cabin. Alex split several stove lengths into smaller pieces that would burn fast. He loaded his arms and stood for a moment, studying the lake, searching for the Beaver.

How had Tom gotten here? He couldn't have walked. No one with his injured leg could make it through that infernal bush. As Alex squinted through the rain, he noticed several items bobbing on the water, far out. One looked like a seat cushion, another some sort of aluminum box.

Had Tom crash-landed the Beaver? Something serious had happened; the older man was in bad shape.

Hurrying inside, Alex stoked the stove, found an overturned bucket and went back out for water. Tom was either asleep or unconscious, his breathing loud and labored. Using his flashlight, Alex searched the unholy mess on the cabin floor, looking for candles and cooking utensils.

He found both, and in a few moments two candles shed flickering light inside the cabin. Soon Alex had his Primus stove going and a small pot of water heating. He used newsprint from a stack beside the stove to clean up the mess beside Tom's bed.

The cabin was warming up fast. When the water boiled, Alex made two mugs of instant cocoa and took one over to the bunk along with a bottle of aspirin from his emergency kit. If the gash on Tom's head had caused concussion, Alex figured it wasn't good to let him sleep. He wasn't sure about giving him aspirin, either, but surely Tom needed something to reduce his fever. He was coughing hard intermittently, and his chest sounded heavy and congested.

Pneumonia? Some kind of flu? There was no way of telling.

"Tom. Hey, Tom, wake up. Sit up and drink this."

It took several tries to finally get Tom to a sitting position. He took the mug, holding it in both hands. Alex steadied it because Tom's hands were shaking violently.

Alex waited until he'd taken the aspirin and drank some of the cocoa. "What happened, Tom? Where's the plane?"

"In the goddamned lake." Tom's voice was barely

a whisper, and it was obviously painful to speak. "Hit a deadhead, the Beaver flipped and sank."

"How long ago?"

Tom frowned and then shook his head. "Don't know."

"Did Bert or Ivy know you were coming here? Did you leave a flight plan with Kisha?" There was no plane to pinpoint his location.

"Nope," Tom wheezed. "Bert's in Anchorage with Kisha. Ivy—" He closed his eyes. "Ivy's mad. She didn't know—I was coming—looking for you. They'll think—probably think I'm fishing."

That was not good news. Alex tried to think of a way to alert someone and came up empty. If Tom had flares they'd be at the bottom of the lake with everything else.

"So nobody knows where you are?" What the hell were they going to do for food, if no one came soon? Was there any salvageable food in the mess the grizzly left? His own supply would get them through a short stay, but they'd eventually run out. And Tom wasn't in any shape to walk.

"Theo. I told him what I was planning."

Alex's spirits lifted. "So Theo knew you were flying out here?"

Tom coughed long and hard before he could answer. "Not when. He knew—I was thinking about it." He took another sip of the hot drink and grimaced when he tried to swallow. "Bloody throat."

"He'll figure it out when you turn up missing." Alex hoped to God he was right. But how long would it be before Theo and the others started putting two and two together? He knew from conversations with Ivy that Tom had always been casual about his flying itinerary. And he wasn't in good shape. He sounded as if he needed a doctor.

"They'll find us." Alex tried to sound optimistic. "In the meantime, I'll get our clothes dry and clean up some of this mess. Was it a grizzly?"

"Didn't see him, thank God. It was like this—when I got here."

"Let's hope he doesn't come back." Alex had the rifle, but he didn't fancy a shoot-out with a grizzly.

"Keep...the fire going." Tom drank the last of the cocoa and slumped down on the bunk, shoving the sleeping bag at Alex. "Take—this," he wheezed. "I'm warm now."

"I will later," Alex lied. "You keep it for now." He shoved it tight around Tom. He had warm clothes, and there was an aluminum emergency blanket at the bottom of his pack. In spite of his claims about being warm, Tom was shivering again, so Alex dug the thin sheet out and encased the other man in it. He used his tent to prop Tom up, hoping that a half-sitting position would make it easier to breathe.

Tom didn't seem to notice. He coughed until his breath was gone, and then lapsed into a drugged sleep that soon became delirium. At one point he shouted, startling Alex, and then struggled to get up, cursing when Alex restrained him. It was a long time before he quieted again.

When Tom finally settled, Alex did what he could with the mess, using a brush he found in a cupboard. Flour, sugar and oatmeal were mixed into a soup all over the floor. A plastic jar of honey was torn in two, the contents licked clean, the sticky residue everywhere. Alex was able to salvage two cans of evaporated milk and two more of beans that had escaped the bear.

As he worked, he tried to figure out why Tom would have been so determined to find him. To warn him away from Ivy? It was the only reason he could think of, but Tom could have done that back in Valdez. Why follow him here?

Alex was yawning by now. He stoked the fire again, unrolled his own sopping clothes from the plastic he'd wrapped them in, hanging them beside Tom's pants and shirt, which were sending off clouds of steam beside the roaring stove.

Tom was alternately snoring and coughing. The wool blanket had slipped to the floor, and because Tom seemed warm enough, Alex wrapped up in it in the second bunk.

He'd have to make sure he stayed half awake. He had to keep the fire going, and he also needed to keep an eye on Tom. Alex was still thinking about the irony of Tom's being here when he fell asleep, sudden and deep.

He woke with a start sometime later when Tom fell.

"Gotta go to the outhouse," he mumbled when Alex hauled him up.

"Okay, let's get your boots on." Alex sat the other man on the bunk and with some difficulty shoved Tom's bare feet into wet leather boots.

Getting the other man to his feet took some maneuvering. Alex finally looped one of Tom's arms around his neck and heaved, supporting most of his weight. Outside, Tom had to stop several times, bending double and leaning heavily against Alex before he caught his breath enough to go on.

"Hell of a note when a guy…can't take a piss under his own steam," he wheezed.

"Maybe you can repay the favor someday," Alex said, adding in an undertone, "I hope to hell not, though."

Tom managed a chuckle as Alex helped him the rest of the way, noting that it was already getting lighter. His watch said 5:00 a.m., and the birds were chirping a mad chorus in the trees. Somewhere to the north several coyotes yipped and a wolf howled, the drawn-out sound eerie in the gray dawn.

Back inside, Alex settled Tom again and then scooped hot water from the bucket on top of the stove. He mixed in a cube of beef broth and got Tom to drink it. Tom was restless, coughing and shivering, but he didn't want to sleep. Instead he propped his back higher against the tent, struggling against the racking cough that took his breath away.

He said in a wheezing whisper, "I feel rotten, real bad chest, sore lungs, one hell of a headache. This is a fine mess I got us into. While I'm awake I gotta talk to you."

"Lie down and rest," Alex urged. "We'll talk about it later, when you're feeling better."

"Don't...give me...that shit." Tom's voice held a trace of his old spirit. "Half the time I'm out of my head with fever, right now I'm not. I came here to talk to you about your father, I'm gonna do it now while my head's clear." He had to stop and struggle for breath.

Alex frowned at him. "I thought you told me about him already."

"Not all of it." Tom coughed again, long and racking.

Alex got him another cup of hot water, and shook three more aspirin out of the bottle. "Maybe these'll help your throat."

Tom swallowed them with difficulty. "There was more than I said. See, Nolan and I got into it hot and heavy that morning. Over Vietnam." He had to keep pausing, but Alex didn't interrupt. He sat down close beside the bunk, listening as closely as he'd ever listened to anyone.

"I'd just gotten back from Cambodia," Tom said. "Damned leg was giving me hell. Nolan was Canadian, what we used to call a peacenik. He said some things about America's involvement over there that made me good and mad. We got into it pretty good. Upshot was, I slammed on the brakes. Told him to get out of my truck."

Tom coughed again and Alex waited. His heart was hammering.

"Left him there by the side of the road, middle of nowhere." Tom's thin voice held half a lifetime of regret. He coughed again, and when he could speak, he said, "It was starting to snow. Should have gone back after I calmed down, but I didn't. Too mad, too stubborn." He swiped weakly at the sweat trickling off his forehead. "Too young, too stupid." He lifted a hand and then let it drop down on the sleeping bag. "Didn't stop at the Park Service or tell the state troopers about Nolan, either, like I should have. Let him walk off into the bush, hardly any supplies, green as grass, no bloody idea what he was getting into."

So that was it. Tom felt responsible for Nolan's death. Alex thought that over. In light of the days he'd just spent struggling through the bush, he could better understand the Alaskan concept of responsibility. But still…

"He was an adult," Alex said at last. "You weren't responsible for what he did. It was his choice."

Tom looked at him through weary, bloodshot eyes. "Horse shit. Up here, everybody's responsible. You don't send your worst enemy off into the bush without proper supplies. Even well equipped, you can go a mile, two miles out, never be found again."

Alex knew that was the truth. He'd had moments the past few days out on the trail when he figured that was going to be his own fate.

"What was Roy really like?"

"Lot like you. Stubborn. Liberal. Quiet spoken, but wouldn't back down. Intelligent, not practical. Useless dreamer. Hopeless idealist with a death wish." He gave a sound meant to be a laugh. "Ivy wouldn't like me saying that. She's forever trying to rub off my rough edges."

The mention of Ivy brought a poignant ache to Alex's heart.

CHAPTER TWENTY-FOUR

There's so many things I've screwed up between us, Lindy. Funny how I can only see that now I'm far away from you.

From letters written by Roy Nolan,
April, 1972

BEFORE HE COULD STOP himself, Alex blurted, "Why did you tell Frances that Ivy was in love with me? How could you know that?"

Tom raised his head, surprise in his bloodshot eyes. "Plain as the nose on your face. You—you talked to Frances?"

Alex nodded. "She introduced herself, in Valdez. She's a very beautiful woman. Classy, and nice into the bargain."

Tom's expression softened. "Always was, always will be." It sounded like a prayer.

Alex took a deep breath. "I feel exactly the same about Ivy, Tom. She's beautiful. She's classy, and I love her." It felt validating to say it out loud.

"She know that?"

"No. Not yet. I didn't know myself until I left the lodge."

"Dumb damn thing to do, walk away without telling her. Her heart was right there on her sleeve, showed every time she said your name."

It hurt that he hadn't wanted to know. It didn't help to be told he was stupid. "If—" he corrected himself quickly "—*when* I get back, I'm going to do my damnedest to get her to marry me." His voice hardened. "I know you don't have much use for me, Pierce, but that's just something we'll both have to live with."

"Maybe, maybe not. Depends on whether I make it out of here." Tom's wheezy voice grew angry. "You plan on taking her south? Because it won't work, Ladrovik. Ivy's roots go deep in Alaska. Rip them loose and she'll suffer."

"Her, or you, Tom?" Alex was fuming. "How can she know what suits her if she's never tried anything else? You've tied her to you with flying and the business, you've used love and the sense of responsibility she feels for you to keep her with you. God, she figures you're a combination of—of Clint Eastwood and—and, I don't know, double oh seven."

"Not any more." Tom seemed to collapse, but Alex wasn't stopping. He was on a roll, had to say everything he'd been thinking. "Maybe Alaska is the right place for Ivy, but she needs to compare it to something else before she knows for sure." He got to his feet and strode the length of the small cabin and back, stopping beside the bunk. "But you'd do everything in your power to prevent that, because you need her close." He expected a barrage, even sick as Tom was.

"You're right about one thing, I don't want to lose her." The stark words were poignant, drawn from Tom's heart. "She's all I've got left now."

Alex pitied the older man, but Ivy needed to be free. "If she agrees to marry me, I don't know where we'll go," he said. "I need to talk to her before I even speculate about things like that. Even if she doesn't want me, she shouldn't have to feel responsible for your happiness, Tom."

To Alex's amazement, Tom slowly nodded. Then he coughed again, harsh and deep. When he got his breath, he said, "Frances is leaving me, she tell you that?"

"No, Ivy did." Alex was weary. He slumped down in the chair again. "Frances didn't tell me anything like that. She said she had to go away, for herself." He leaned forward, trying to make the older man understand, but also justifying his own actions. "Like I had to make this trip, for reasons of my own. I understood exactly what she meant." Alex tried to put it into words. "I couldn't get any perspective on my life back in San Diego. After my daughter died, I went a little nuts. My marriage broke up, I quit my job. I didn't give a damn about anything, not even my own life."

Tom's gaze was intense. "How old was your girl?"

"Three. Her name was Annie."

"I didn't know you lost a kid. Sorry for your loss. Ivy tell you her brother died? Years ago now. My boy was older than Ivy, five when he passed."

"Ivy told me about Jacob. That's how I understand why Frances needs to go away."

"She fell apart afterwards." Tom seemed to be having more and more trouble getting air into his lungs. "Then I did this stupid thing…."

Tom stopped speaking and Alex waited. They had plenty of time.

"I had an affair with a woman I grew up with. Thought nobody would know, bloody fool me. As if there's any secrets in Valdez. Frances found out, and that finished her off. Depression, they call it now. The old doctor in Valdez called it a nervous breakdown."

"Ivy told me."

Tom's eyebrows shot up.

"About the depression, not the affair." At this moment, he felt deeply sorry for Tom. Just as he understood how Frances had reacted, so, too, he could easily understand Tom's actions. Grief was an unpredictable thing; it made slaves of its victims.

"Seems like you two hit it off, you and Frances." There was more than a trace of resentment and bitterness in Tom's voice.

"We did. But when she told me Ivy was in love

with me, I panicked. See, after Annie, after my marriage collapsed, I got it in my head that I wouldn't let myself care about anyone again. That way, nothing could hurt that bad."

Tom thought about it and finally nodded. "Guess I was luckier than you. I already had Ivy. How could I stop caring about her?" He was chilled again, shivering and visibly exhausted. Alex shouldn't have kept him talking for so long.

"You'd better get some sleep, Tom. Give those aspirin a chance to work."

"In a minute. Look here, I need to say some things. Don't know if I'm going to make it out of here, and I have to get this off my chest."

The quiet words were alarming, because on some level Alex had suspected that Tom was giving up. There was no question he was very ill.

"Of course you're going to make it, Ivy will be searching for you any minute now. Then we'll get you to hospital."

"I want you to tell Ivy this for me. Say that she's to do whatever her heart says to do. If you two get married, she has my blessing. All I want is for her to be happy."

He coughed again, and his body shook with the effort. It took longer to get his breath again, and he slid down farther on the bunk.

"Frances knows I love her. Tell her I said good

luck with her plans, her new job. I was an asshole, but I always loved her."

"I'll tell them both what you said. Get some sleep now." Alex tucked the sleeping bag and the aluminum sheet tighter around Tom. When the other man's eyes closed and his rapid, uneven breathing slowed, Alex stirred a spoonful of instant coffee into a mug of hot water and sat in the chair, trying to figure out what he could do.

Tom was in bad shape. The weather might make it impossible to fly, so it could be several more days or even a week before Ivy was able to look for her father. With no sign of the floatplane, she'd likely pass right over the cabin. Of course he'd go outside and try to flag her down if he heard the copter, but after the way he'd left, she might not be at all eager to see him. There was no way to let her know that Tom was inside.

Alex wasn't about to let Tom die if he could help it, but he couldn't leave the other man and go for help. Tom wasn't well enough to even keep the fire going. And Alex shuddered at the thought of back-tracking over the trail. But by sitting here day after day, their food supplies would dwindle fast. There were fish in the lake and probably moose and caribou out in the bush, but Alex was no hunter. Fisherman, either. It would be pure blind luck if he ever landed something edible.

There was always the possibility that someone might come to use the cabin, but this early in the year, that was a very faint hope. He couldn't trust to chance, there wasn't time. Tom needed medical attention, and he needed it soon. Alex had to come up with some foolproof way to attract attention.

If Ivy's father died, she'd never forgive him. She'd always believe there was something he could have done. And he'd believe it, too.

Alex got up and shoved more wood in the stove. It was the leaping flames that gave him the idea.

He had to start a fire big enough to attract attention from a long ways off.

CHAPTER TWENTY-FIVE

Kiss the little guy for me. And for you, lots more than kisses. I love you, Linda.

From letters written by Roy Nolan,
April, 1972

"WHERE'S TOM?" Bert signed when Ivy came into the office on Friday afternoon.

Ivy shrugged her shoulders and raised her hands, palms up. The weather had cleared overnight and she'd just gotten back from dropping fishermen and their guide at a remote creek. They were due to be picked up in two days, and they wanted Tom to come and get them with the Beaver. Ivy knew they viewed him as a colorful Alaskan character, someone they could describe at dinner parties. She and the copter weren't nearly as interesting, and also the float was a lot cheaper to charter.

"He told Kisha he was staying at one of the camps along the Katalla until the storm blew over. He's probably fishing. We tried to raise him on the radio, but there's no answer. Kisha's trying to get hold of the fishing camp, but nobody's answering there, either."

"He should be here now," Bert insisted.

Amen to that.

"How long he's gone?"

Ivy added it up. "Three days now. Maybe four." Longer than she'd realized. A twinge of anxiety came and went. He'd been away that long before. If the fish were biting, he'd probably lost track of time.

Bert frowned. "He promised I would solo this morning. He wouldn't forget—important day for us. We should go looking, maybe engine trouble."

"He'd have radioed if he was having problems." But Ivy remembered the day the radio had conked out on the copter. Could that have happened to the Beaver? Her uneasiness was now becoming real concern. She'd been too angry and distracted to focus on the fact that there'd been no contact with Tom. Usually he'd have radioed in at least once, to give his location and check on schedules.

"What was his last contract, Kisha?"

"He was doing the milk run." The girl riffled through the stack of papers and handed one to Ivy. Sure enough, it was his regular fishing camp route. The last contact he'd made was the day after he'd dropped Ivy at the lodge, which was Tuesday morning.

"Maybe he decided to visit some old crony. Uncle

Theo might know." She used the radio phone, relieved when Sage picked up.

"Hey, are you coming up?" her cousin said. "We need a good long visit soon."

Ivy had deliberately avoided going to the lodge the past couple days. She'd found it uncomfortable being around Mavis, and she wasn't ready to confide in Sage. Not yet. First she needed to get used to everything herself. Frances was the only one Ivy could talk to easily these days, and they'd been spending time together, a development that still amazed her. Probably amazed Frances, too.

Ivy apologized to Sage. "Not today. Tom's away, I'm super busy here. Sage, could you ask Theo if Dad told him exactly where he was going the other day? We're a little concerned here because he hasn't been in touch."

Sage immediately understood. Her voice sharp, she didn't ask any more questions. "I'll find Theo and call you right back."

Seven minutes later the phone rang.

Without preamble, Sage said, "Your dad was taking his usual route up the Katalla river. And he told Theo he was thinking of tracking Alex down at one of the public cabins up in the Chugach, but he didn't say exactly when." Sage gave Ivy the exact location of the cabin.

Ivy wondered if she'd heard right. *Why would Tom go looking for Alex?*

"What's going on, Ivy? Is there anything we can do?"

Ivy kept her tone light. "Dad's been out of touch for a couple of days, you know how he does that sometimes. I wasn't too worried, but Bert thinks he should have come back to Valdez this morning. I'm going to buzz up to that cabin in the Chugach, see if I can spot the Beaver."

"Let us know as soon as you locate him."

Ivy promised. She hung up and told Bert where she was going.

"I can come?" His concern showed on his face. "Please."

She'd thought she wanted to be alone, but now she realized she'd be glad to have Bert along. "Absolutely. Two sets of eyes are better than one."

They were airborne within minutes.

AT THE CABIN, the morning was half gone before Alex admitted that he wasn't going to be able to light the series of bonfires he'd planned along the lakeshore. The wood he'd laboriously gathered from the forest was soaked with the recent rain, and he didn't have an unlimited supply of matches. There was no gasoline or starter that would make wet wood burn more easily. Hard as he tried, the stacks of wood he lit fizzled and went out.

Why the hell hadn't he ever been a Boy Scout?

In between attempts, Alex kept the stove hot in the cabin, checking often on Tom, who'd lapsed again into a fevered half-delirious state. He slapped fretfully at the cup of hot tea Alex tried to get him to drink, spilling it on the mattress. He wouldn't swallow more aspirin, and he mumbled incoherently, calling out for Frances. He needed medical attention, and he needed it soon.

Outside it was starting to rain again. If only there was enough dry wood to get a big fire going, maybe someone would notice it. Alex looked around the clearing. There was the cabin, he could set that on fire, but if help didn't arrive, then he and Tom would be without shelter.

Bad idea, Ladrovik.

His gaze swept past the outhouse, and then he zeroed in on it. It was far enough from the cabin that it wouldn't pose a threat. The logs it was constructed from were relatively dry. It should burn, if he could just get it going. And although it was convenient, it wasn't absolutely necessary to their survival.

With his hatchet, Alex chopped firewood into kindling. Carefully, he laid the makings for a fire on the wooden floor just inside the outhouse, adding bigger and bigger pieces of dry firewood. When the flames began to lick at the walls, he left the door open so oxygen would feed them. He wiped the sweat away from his face. His hand came away black with soot.

"Please," he whispered as the flames grew. "Ivy, beloved, please come and find us soon."

"FIRE." Bert mouthed the word and pointed, but Ivy had already spotted it. Something was burning at the camp, something big. As they drew nearer, she realized it wasn't the cabin.

"No Beaver," Bert signed, and Ivy nodded. She'd had a sick feeling in her belly ever since they took off, and now she felt worse. She made a pass over the cabin, looking for a suitable landing spot and, when she did, she saw Alex. He came bursting out of the cabin and began running up and down the lakeshore, urgently waving his coat at her. Something was obviously wrong. She scanned the area, but there was no sign of Tom or the Beaver.

Landing here wasn't going to be easy because of the slope dropping down to the lake. She circled, looking for a suitable spot, finally deciding on a meadow a quarter mile from the cabin.

Her heart in her throat, Ivy set the copter down. She and Bert were running toward the cabin when Alex burst out of the woods.

When he got close enough he pulled Ivy into his arms. He was panting hard and looked wild and unkempt. There was soot on his hands and face, and his thick dark beard scratched her cheek. He smelled of wood smoke and sweat, and she could feel his heart pounding.

She let him hold her for a moment before she pulled away.

"What's going on, Alex?"

"Thank God you came, Ivy," he said when he got his breath. "I knew you would. Tom's back at the cabin," he said, signing so Bert would understand. "He hit a deadhead when he was landing the Beaver. The plane's at the bottom of the lake." He paused to catch his breath again. "He's really sick. He hit his head getting out of the plane, gashed it pretty deep. He's delirious—I think he may have pneumonia, but I don't know." The words tumbled out. "He's coughing really bad, having trouble breathing. He needs medical attention fast."

"Let's go." Ivy took off at a trot, the men following her.

Tom was coherent when they reached the cabin, but he wasn't strong enough to sit up. Ivy knelt beside the bunk.

"Hey, Captain, how's it going?" She was profoundly shocked at how weak and sick he was, how old he looked. When he tried to say something, she shushed him.

"Conserve your energy, we'll have lots of time to

talk later," she said, choking back tears. "Right now, we're going to get you to the hospital." It was confirmation to her of how sick he was that Tom didn't even try to argue.

Tom was wearing only a pair of Alex's track pants, and together they got him into a shirt. By the time they were done, Bert had cut two sturdy poles to make a stretcher, and he and Alex lashed them together with pieces of rope cut from Alex's backpack. They secured the woolen blanket over the frame, and it took all three of them to bundle Tom into Alex's sleeping bag. When that was done, they wrapped the aluminum blanket around him and lifted him onto the makeshift stretcher.

Alex and Bert carried him to the copter. Ivy brought up the rear with Alex's backpack. She'd spent a few moments wondering if he'd stay behind, doggedly pursuing his father's odyssey. She finally said to him, as casually as she could manage, "Are you coming with us, Alex?"

He looked squarely at her, his eyes weary and bloodshot behind his glasses. "Damned right I'm coming. I've done everything I came here to do. And if I never spend another night in this bush it'll be too soon. Even a helicopter ride is better than that."

"This one's going to be fast and furious. You want a bucket in case you get sick?"

"I'm over being afraid."

There wasn't time to ask him what had happened. They settled Tom as best they could in the back of the copter. Bert sat beside him, supporting him. Alex climbed in beside Ivy. Before she began her preflight check, she radioed Kisha and asked her to call the Valdez hospital, giving them an ETA for arrival at the helipad at Up And Away and asking for an ambulance to meet them.

And then Ivy put everything out of her mind except flying.

CHAPTER TWENTY-SIX

I saw them, Linda. The Northern Lights. It was about midnight. One of the other guys in the hostel woke me up. I swear I heard them, like a swishing sound. It's something I'll never forget if I live to be a hundred.

From letters written by Roy Nolan,
April, 1972

AT THE HELIPAD in Valdez, medics were waiting with a stretcher. They suggested that Alex go along in the ambulance to tell the doctors what had happened and to give them some idea of Tom's symptoms during the past several days, so Ivy and Bert followed in her truck.

Alex met them when they walked through the automatic doors. He took Ivy's hand and threaded his fingers through hers.

"They took him in there—" Alex indicated the emergency area "—but nobody's said anything yet about how he is."

The three of them waited anxiously until finally a young and pretty E.R. doctor came out and reported on Tom's condition. After she'd established who they all were, she said, "I'm Doctor Carrie Rothel," offering her hand to Ivy. "We've done some X-rays on your dad. He has pneumonia and he's dehydrated and very weak. Does he have an allergy to penicillin?"

"Not that I know of," Ivy said.

"Good. He's had a severe blow to the skull. But there's no sign of fracture, and the wound has already begun to heal. Do you know if he lost consciousness afterwards?"

"I don't know," Ivy said. "He was in a floatplane that was upside down and sinking under water. If he'd been knocked unconscious for very long he would have drowned." Until this moment, she hadn't had time to think clearly about what had happened to Tom. The full import came to her now. "He's lucky to be alive," she whispered, trembling. What if he'd died? They'd parted on such terrible terms. She'd never have forgiven herself.

Alex put his arm came around her shoulders in a reassuring hug. Then he signed to Bert what the doctor had said.

"We've started an IV drip to get fluids into him, and we'll get him on penicillin for the pneumonia," the doctor said. "We'll be taking him up to Intensive Care shortly, the nurses are just cleaning him up a little first. As soon as they're done you can see him. In the meantime the admissions desk will have forms for you to fill out," she added.

"I have to phone my mother," Ivy said. And she should also have Kisha call the lodge on the radio phone.

"There's a pay phone just down the hall." The doctor pointed it out.

Alex walked with her.

Ivy dialed, and when her mother answered she shoved money in the slot with shaking fingers, and then quickly explained what had happened.

"I'll be there right away," Frances said. Ivy heard her quavering intake of breath. "Tell Tom I'm on my way."

"Drive carefully, Mom." But Frances had hung up before Ivy finished speaking. Next, she dialed Up And Away, repeating what she'd told her mother. Kisha promised to call the lodge immediately.

Alex was just a few feet away, waiting for her. He took her hand and led her to the waiting room. There were only two other people there besides Bert, plump, middle-aged women who looked enough alike to be twins. Alex had chosen seats as far away from them as possible, and Ivy, panicking, realized he wanted to have a private discussion with her. She really didn't want to hear what he had to say. She was on emotional overload, and she wasn't sure she could handle one more thing.

"I need to fill in forms," she said, pulling her hand away from his. "I need to see Dad." When she turned toward the door, Alex stopped her by taking both her hands, holding on hard. "Ivy, please give me a moment. I need to get some things straight with you. I'm so sorry for leaving you the way I did."

She knew she should play it cool, but she had nothing left in her for game playing. "You should be sorry," she said loudly. The two women turned their heads her way, and even Bert was watching.

In spite of her best intentions at staying neutral, tears sprang to her eyes and all the rage and resentment she felt spilled out. "You dumped me, and you didn't even say goodbye." She made no attempt at lowering her voice. "You went rushing off as if I was some—some one-night stand you couldn't wait to get rid of." Her voice rose even higher. "You put your stupid Jeep ahead of me. How could you treat me like that?"

"My Jeep?" He looked puzzled. "I know I didn't do the right thing, leaving the way I did, and I apologize, but I don't get the Jeep part."

That infuriated her. "You said you'd be back for your Jeep, and you might *just* have time to see me before you took off south. Words to that effect. *Now* do you remember?"

The two women weren't even pretending not to listen. Good, she had witnesses, Ivy fumed.

"God, I'm such a jerk." He closed his eyes and

blew out a long breath. "Ivy, forgive me, please. I'm a total idiot. I was so scared to let myself care for you. It was like a virus I couldn't shake. All I could do was walk away. I hadn't gone far before I realized I'd made an awful mistake, the worst mistake of my life." His voice deepened. "I love you, Ivy. Before I even try to explain, I want you to know that."

The words yanked at her heartstrings, but she wasn't ready to let him know. "Oh, yeah? You love me, huh? And why should I believe you?"

She heard one of the women say, "Right on, sister."

Bert just looked confused. "Fight?" he signed.

Ivy nodded. "Damned right," she mouthed in his direction.

Alex's glasses were so dirty it was a miracle he could even see her. "You know I'm telling you the truth," he said softly. "I may be an idiot, but I've never lied to you, Ivy."

She thought that over and reluctantly had to admit it was true. He'd told her the truth even when she didn't want to hear it. But she needed time to digest this new truth of his. And there were so many things she needed to know. The first was one she couldn't even guess at. It had been plaguing her ever since she'd talked with Sage. She wrapped her arms around her midriff and said, "*Why* did my dad come looking for you, anyway?"

"Because he needed to tell me about meeting my father."

She frowned. “I thought he told you. That day in the office.”

Alex shook his head. “Not all of it. According to Tom, they had an argument, your father and mine. That day Tom picked Roy up? They fought over Vietnam, if you can believe it. Tom says Roy was opinionated, stubborn and idealistic.”

“Like father, like son.”

“Probably. Things got pretty heated, and Tom stopped the truck and ordered Roy out, pretty much in the middle of nowhere, in a snowstorm. Tom’s always felt guilty.”

One of the women said, “Oh, my.”

Ivy nodded slowly. “I can see why Dad felt guilty. Especially after your father went missing.”

Alex shook his head. “It wasn’t Tom’s fault Nolan died.”

“No, it wasn’t.” Ivy couldn’t help but see the irony of Alex defending her father. But she understood far better than Alex the law of the Arctic.

If it hadn’t been for Bert, she, too, might have had to live with the same agonizing guilt. She might have waited too long before she went looking for Tom.

Her father’s actions hadn’t been heroic. Her beloved Captain was only human. He’d made serious mistakes and lived to regret them.

She’d done that herself, with her mother. It hurt to remember how cruel she’d been to Frances. Seeing

Tom so close to death today, she'd also learned that harboring anger and resentment was dangerous. You could forever lose the opportunity to let someone know you loved them, no matter what they'd done.

No matter what they hadn't done.

She opened her mouth to tell Alex that in spite of everything, she loved him, but her mother interrupted before she could get the words out.

CHAPTER TWENTY-SEVEN

You know what I've always said about marriage, Lindy, that it isn't for me. But a guy's got a right to change his mind. When I get back we'll talk about it.

From the last letter written by Roy Nolan,
April, 1972

"IVY?" Frances hurried over to them. Ivy wrapped her arms around her mother. For a long moment, they held each other.

Feeling this close to her mother, being physically demonstrative with her, was still new, and Ivy marveled at the comfort it gave her. Frances greeted Alex and Bert, and then turned back to Ivy.

"I spoke to the doctor—she said we can see Tom now. He has pneumonia and a concussion. What happened, Ivy? I didn't even know he was overdue on a flight."

"Neither did I." Shame sent color flaming in Ivy's face. "I thought he'd holed up because of the storm and gone fishing. I feel so bad for just assuming that."

Frances shook her head and hugged Ivy again. "He went off on his own in the Beaver all the time, how could you know this time was any different? Tell me exactly what happened."

Ivy stuck to the facts, saying only that Tom had gone to look for Alex. There'd be time enough later to fill her mother in on all the reasons for that.

"Tom must have followed procedure exactly," she said. She didn't need to add that otherwise he wouldn't be around. Her mother knew enough about planes to understand that very well.

"He hit his head," Ivy went on, "probably when the plane hit. But somehow he made it to the cabin. Alex found him a day or so later."

"There wasn't a lot I could do, apart from keeping him warm and making hot drinks," Alex explained. "All I had with me was aspirin."

"And then you lit the outhouse—you saved his life," Ivy said. She hadn't fully appreciated that until right now.

Alex smiled at her. His teeth were very white against his dark beard. They were the only part of him that looked clean. "You think they're going to charge me with arson?"

Before Ivy could reply, one of the women who'd been listening said in a booming voice, "My son's a lawyer, and a darned good one. If they try anything like that, you just call him, young man. Here's his card." With some effort, she struggled to her feet and thrust it into Alex's hand. "Arson, indeed. Why, sounds to me like you're a hero." She turned to Ivy. "And excuse me for butting in, young lady, but I think you should just let bygones be bygones."

"Cut him a break, honey," the other woman agreed. "My goodness, this is more exciting than *Days Of Our Lives*."

Ivy started to giggle and couldn't stop.

She'd barely regained control of herself when Doctor Fredricks strode through the door. He put a large hand on Ivy's shoulder, extending his other to Frances. "Ivy, hi. Hello, Frances. Carrie just told me that Tom's in ICU, if there's anything I can do—?"

Ivy looked up at him. He really was a good-looking man, very tall and dark and handsome, distinguished-looking in his sharply pressed khakis and button-down checked shirt. Clean, very clean.

Too bad he hadn't rung any bells for her. Things would have been a lot easier. "Thanks, Dylan, it's good of you to offer. But Doctor Rothel's been great. She said we could go see Dad soon."

Dylan nodded. "Carrie's the best, she'll make sure everything goes well. And I'll keep tabs on Tom for you as well."

"He's going to try and sign himself out the moment he can walk," Frances warned.

Dylan gave her a warm, reassuring smile. "Don't worry about that, we'll use restraints if we have to."

Alex was interpreting for Bert, and Ivy noticed that he was the only one who didn't smile at Dylan's little joke. She also noted that he wasn't too pleased about the arm Dylan had casually snaked around her shoulders.

"Dylan Fredricks, this is Alex Ladrovik," Ivy said. "And you know Bert."

Dylan nodded and smiled at the other two men.

"Alex found Dad after his plane went into the lake," Ivy added.

"Pleasure to meet you, Alex." Dylan extended an antiseptically clean, well-cared-for hand, nails short and manicured. He still managed to keep one arm around Ivy.

"And you." Alex's hand with its broken nails and raw scratches looked as if it had done hard, dirty work very recently. All of him looked that way, Ivy concluded.

And she knew for a fact he didn't smell anything like the expensive aftershave that wafted from Dylan.

Alex was definitely her kind of man. She reached up and took Dylan's hand in hers for a moment, enjoying the narrow-eyed glare Alex gave both of them. A little jealousy wasn't a bad thing.

"Would you like some coffee, or maybe lunch?" Dylan said. "I'm just heading down to the cafeteria."

The invitation included everyone, but Ivy suspected it was meant for her. She decided to put Alex out of his misery.

"Thanks, Dylan, but we're going to see Dad now." She slid out from under his arm and reached a hand out to Alex, threading her fingers through his. She knew the conclusions Dylan would draw from that, and a glance at his face proved she was right.

"Coming, Alex?"

"Absolutely." The force of his grip on her fingers made her wince.

Tom was allowed one visitor at a time, for ten minutes only, so Frances went first. When Ivy's turn came, she was shocked all over again at how frail Tom appeared, propped high on pillows, tubes in his veins, oxygen prongs in his nostrils. His breathing was shallow and so obviously difficult she suddenly felt as if she, too, couldn't get a deep breath.

"Hey, Captain. Don't try to talk. I—I just wanted you to know that I love you, and I'm so glad you got out when the Beaver sank." Her voice was wobbly. "You'll have to tell me exactly how you did that. I remember studying it but it's a tricky maneuver. For now, though, just concentrate on getting better, okay?" She leaned over and kissed his stubbly cheek.

Tears welled in Tom's blue eyes. "Lost—the Beaver. Lost—everything." His voice was almost gone, and it was obviously an effort to speak. Ivy wiped his tears away with a tissue.

"No, you didn't. Not everything. Not even close. As for the Beaver, we'll get another one. We've got insurance, remember?"

He tried to smile at her, but the effort was too much.

"That—yahoo of yours," he whispered.

"Alex?" For a moment, she tensed, wondering what Tom was going to say. And then she relaxed. She didn't really care anymore what her father thought of Alex, Ivy realized. She didn't care what anyone thought. The only thing that mattered was what she felt.

"He's—good people, Ivy. Give him a chance."

Coming from Tom, it was high praise.

"Chance, hell. He's right out of chances. I'm going to hogtie him and get him to the altar before he runs away again." It would take some adjustment on both sides, but she figured they could manage that.

"Good girl. About time," he breathed. His eyes shut. Ivy smiled and brushed the thinning hair back from his forehead and, after a moment, she tiptoed out.

Alex was waiting for her. He'd washed up while she was in with Tom. It was an improvement, but it was going to take more than a hospital bathroom to really make a difference. But she'd learned that heroes came in all sorts of disguises.

"How is he?" Behind his glasses, his dark eyes were weary.

"He's going to be okay. Why don't we go home, Alex? I've got a bathtub and lots of hot water. I might even have a razor somewhere."

"Home?" He gave her a puzzled look.

"To my place. You've never seen my house. You'll like it. You can clean up and then take me somewhere nice for dinner." She glanced at his clothes. "First we'll stop off at The Prospector and get you some clothes."

"No, Ivy." He glanced around. There was no one nearby. "We're not putting this off any longer. Roy never asked my mother to marry him until it was too late. He got around to talking about it in the very last letter he wrote her. He walked away from love, Ivy. He died before he could remedy his mistake. I followed in his footsteps long enough to know that walking away isn't what I want. I want you."

And then he did something that astonished her. Alex dropped to one knee on the shiny floor, oblivious to the amused glances of two nurses passing by and an orderly pushing an empty stretcher.

"I love you, Ivy. I want to have kids with you. If that means making Alaska home and riding around in that damned helicopter with you, I'll give it my best shot. So will you marry me?"

She ought to make him suffer a little, but summer

was coming. It was the best time to get married in Alaska. All the locals knew that the long winter darkness was the perfect time for making babies.

Dearest Tom—

Just a note to confirm that I'll be arriving in Anchorage on Friday, April 9, Alaskan Airlines flight 270. I can't wait to see our grandson, those hospital photos never do them justice. My job is all I dreamed it would be, but I miss you, Tom. And I never thought I'd say this, but I also miss Valdez. We have a lot to talk about, and so much to celebrate. See you soon. Frances.